Short Stories #1

Other books by
Wyatt Knight

Ana's Real Lover
Brothers and their Wives
Clear Eyes
Dan's Worst Best man
Deep South
Deeper South Vol. 1^2
Destiny's Wild Spree Vol 1
Amy Learns the Truth Vol.2
"From a Crushed Carnation to a Lotus Flower"
Gale's Dream Farm
Hear the Wind Blow
Jack and Jill
New and Used

Marcy's Dark Affair
Sweet Bitterness a series
Part 1 The Beginning of Sweet Bitterness
Part 2 Going to the New World
Part 3 Off to War, like Hell
Part 4 Hot Girls on the Farm
Part 5 Hot Women Troubles
Part 6 Misery and Ultimate Joy
Part 7 A New Life
Part 8 Hot Women in the Family
Part 9 Bad dreams, Heartaches: Good Outcomes
The Clearing in the Forest
Part 1   Bawdy and Nice
Part 2   There are changes coming to
those on Hall's Mountain
Part 3   There's a Clearing in everyone's
Forest
Love Goddesses a series
Part 1 The Adventure Begins
Part 2 Love is Close to Home
Part 3 Les Makes a Return Trip to see Miss Tight Ass
Part 4 Rebecca's New Release on Life
Part 5   Les Finds True Love
Short Stories:
Stories of Love and More

Contents

Book 1- Take Me With You

Book 2- Daughters like Mother

Take Me With You

He sat waiting to meet someone from his past, that was all he knew of the person he was to meet. He couldn't think of anyone from his past that he cared to meet but he was curious of who it was. A voice said I hope I haven't made you wait to long. He turned to see who was talking and he remembered her from another time in his life that he didn't wish to think about. He stood and said my you sure have taken good care of yourself. Yes she said hard work tends to help. He said sit down if you are here to meet with me. Yes that is the reason I'm here after all theses years. He said do you want to order. No she said, you may if you wish, but I came to meet and talk to you. Now we will begin, first I had a PI track you down and I set a limit about how far he could go in to your life as you are. I told him what I wanted and to know and to not to get into your personal life. Arthur, first please if you will tel I me about your family but not to personal. She said tell me all you wish about your life since you walked away from me. Hanna when I walked away I felt it was the best for both of us. I made my way to this city and found work in an electronic store. I had no money and no place to stay. The owner of the store was a good man and he let me live in a room at the the store. I ran the store and made a profit for the man. His health wasn't the best but he wouldn't slow down. I had a room and after sometime I was a regular for their Sunday dinners. I went for dinner one Sunday and he introduced me to a woman that was his Daughter. She was a very kind and loving woman who had been to college and had become a nurse. She had been in a poverty stricken country helping doctors care for all they could overcome hunger and sickness. To make it short we fell in love and married. By this time I had helped open up a chain of electronic stores for my now Father in law. My wife Elaine stayed busy working at local hospitals doing volunteer work. We hoped to have children but it wasn't happening. My Father-in-law passed first and that put me over all of the stores we had. Time passed and my Mother-in-law passed leaving all the stores and assets to Elaine. I had opened up more stores and I put a general manager over all of the stores. Elaine was worried about not giving me a Son, I told her it would happen if it was God's will. Elaine's health went bad and it had something to do with a virus she had contracted from a village where she was helping out overseas. She slowly went away more each day. She asked for me to find another love that would give me children after she was gone. She passed away leaving me all the family owned, she was all of the family. I took care of the business but I never remarried. Now that's the way my life has been, now what about you Hannah? She said now what I have to say to you I can't tell you here, so you may want to use the restroom, I am. She said I'll meet you up front. Soon they were in a taxi and she said it's a nice day and she gave the driver the address. Soon they were seated on a park bench. She said Mac the words I may use I have to use them to get my feelings out. So let me begin, when I was around ten years old Vanna and I shared the same bedroom. Every night Dad came to our room and went to Vanna's bed. Soon she was all giggly and squeals and laughing. She did a lot of this every night then Dad just went out of the room. I wondered what made Vanna laugh and giggle. The next night after Vanna got her laughs and Dad started to leave the room I asked Dad why did Vanna laugh so much? He said she liked the candy I gave her. I said you never gave me candy. He said I didn't know you wanted any candy. Yes I said Dad I want some candy. He said I'll have some candy for you tomorrow night. After Vanna got candy the next night and laughed Dad came to my bed. He said do you want your candy now? Oh yes I said and he gave me a piece of candy, he said suck on it as I make you laugh. I felt Dad's hands on my little nipples then he was between my legs with his hand as he rubbed my little girl place as he said, oh that feels good. It was a regular thing for me and Vanna. He was doing more with Vanna than me and she did a lot of squealing. Dad was licking and kissing my girl place by now. One night I saw Dad hold up Vanna as he put his dick up in her ass. She laughed and giggled then she fell flat on the bed. I heard Dad say to her to go wash her ass real good. That night Dad tried to push his tongue up in a place that I didn't even know what it was. I told Dad that I didn't want any more of his candy. For some time I watched Vanna and Dad as he put his dick up in her secret places. I asked her after Dad left our room what they were doing? Hanna said Mac I've never used the F word so I'll use the doing it words. Vanna said doing it, that means when a man's dick goes up in your ass. I said and that's the way it's done? No Vanna said Dad does it in my ass so I won't get pregnant. I said does it hurt your ass? No she said Dad's dick is the smallest one I've ever had up my ass or pussy so far. I said Sis what's a pussy? She said Sis it's the hole right below your pee hole, you want me to put my finger in yours? No I said and what Dad's doing can't be right. Vanna said oh Dad's dick won't hurt your ass or pussy. No it won't because Dad or no boy won't get up in me til I get ready. Dad was ready to put his fingers or dick up in my pussy the next night. I told him I didn't want any more of his candy. He said he wanted my ass and my pussy and he was going to get it. She said I used the words that I used to get the bully's away from me at school. I told Dad I would tell my teacher. Dad backed off but dared me to never tell anyone. Vanna and Dad just quit doing it. Vanna just quit doing Dad's dick but she got every boy to do her ass and pussy that she could get. I believe she liked the dick up her ass more than up in her pussy. She would take as many as six boys and men up in her ass or pussy every day. Time passed and I felt bad and dirty for letting Dad do what he had done to me. Sis was doing any man or boy that would do her. I tried talking to her about what she was doing with her ass and pussy, about how wrong it was. Sis had a mind to do what made her feel good she told me. Dad passed and I never cried for him but I felt even more dirtier than ever. I had no one to tell about how I felt about my Dad and all he had done to me and Sis. I began to go to your house and talk to your Mom and Dad. They would sit and listen to me talk about what was on my mind. I didn't just blab to them all at once all that was bothering me. Your Mom said Vanna don't ever feel that you are to blame for what someone does to you. Your Dad said yes and don't go through your life with a guilt for what another person has done wrong with you. Your Mom said it will help you when you tell someone else about it. I began to tell them all I had wanted to tell someone that cared. Your Mom and Dad would sit and listen to what I had to say and they helped me to see what Dad had done wasn't my fault. They helped me to understand the Bible as your Dad would read the Bible. I loved to visit my new Mom and Dad because they cared how I felt about what was right and wrong. The big reason to visit was that I got to be closer to the boy I loved and I hoped to marry, then my Mom, well your Mom died and I was lost without her. I went to see your Dad one day and we sat out on the porch and talked about life and the paths we took. He said sometimes our lives would take a path that we may not choose but it may be God's choice for us. Your Dad went into the house and brought out and handed me a Bible. He said read some every day but ask God to help you understand his holy word. Your Dad gave me my most precious gift up to that time. I wanted to hug your Dad, but I didn't, I thanked him and cried. Your Dad put his arms around me and said Hannah you remember this, there will be times in your life that you will need help and times when you can help. Hannah you will learn that it is better to give than to receive. He said you better get your little butt on home. Mac looks like going to be late getting home. Mac I had never been kissed or wanted to kiss a boy or man in my life but I wanted to kiss and hug this gentle caring man. No I didn't I just told your Dad bye and went home. Your Dad my only friend, died that night,

I cried for this man My Dad. I never shed a tear for my birth Dad. Over time you became the boy that I wanted to marry and grow old with as we loved and I gave you your children. I really felt like you loved me and we would be living out a wonderful happy life together. One night after Vanna had been out screwing any man or boy that would screw her ass or pussy I heard this, Mom said you know Joe has never worked or ever will so you know how to take care of this matter. At the time I didn't know what the matter was. Some time later in the week Mom asked Vanna if she had took care of the matter? Vanna said yes Mom I did but he won't get any more of my pussy, Mom he tore my pussy apart with his big dick. What she said next hurt me bad? Mom said oh Mac's dick couldn't be as large as you say. Vanna said it was my pussy Mac tore up not yours. Mom said well just give Mac enough of your pussy to support you and his baby.

It hurt me that you had screwed Vanna's pussy but it hurt more to know that my man was being tricked into a marriage. I didn't want a baby to grow up without his Father in his life. Yes it hurt that your large dick had screwed Vanna's pussy and not mine, oh I didn't care if your dick had tore her pussy open, not mine. Mac I tried to talk to you about all I had heard but it seemed to me that all I was to you was another snotty nosed little Sister. So here I am getting an old house ready to live in for my Sister and my lover. Yes I got your house ready to live in as Vanna took all the men and boys up in her ass and pussy she could get. Now through all of this I thought our love would win over. I'll move ahead to where Vanna had me to come clean for her sorry ass as she lay in bed, oh yes you were at work. I began to watch one boy or man after another go in the house as I was hid. She screwed from four to six of her lovers, Joe got her last. That one day when you came home early I was up in the attic watching them screw Vanna's ass and pussy. Joe had his dick in Vanna's ass at the time, before you came in she had ass screwed Joe and pussy too. Once she sucked Joe's dick and she swallowed all he shot in her mouth. I don't think they cared about you watching Joe's dick up in Vanna's ass or pussy. I lay up in the attic and cried for the man I loved to see what he had seen. You tried to put Joe out but it was his cousin's house so you had to go they said. I heard Joe and Vanna talk before about her taking your large dick. Joe said to her to let Mac have enough pussy to keep you around. The next thing I know you had divorced Vanna and I thought now Mac is mine. That wasn't the way you saw it. You were leaving and here I am begging you to take me with you. I cried and I begged for you to take me with you. I watched as the man I loved turn and walked away as I lay in the dirt crying for you to please take me with you. I've cried a little every day of my life then I think he has his own life and it's best to not go back in the past. Your Mom and Dad told me to look ahead for a better tomorrow and hope the next day was better than the day before. Vanna's ass and belly grew large and she got lazier. I tried to get her to go out for walks. She only walked far enough to get a dick up in her ass or pussy. I got away from her and Mom by picking berries when they were ripe. Vanna's baby was born and she got lazier than ever. Mom wouldn't help with the baby nor would Vanna. I had the baby all to myself. I did it all for him while Vanna was out with her lovers. Mom, she was as lazy or worse than Vanna. I had me a baby to take care of without any help at all. It was summer and I had made me a back pack to carry my baby. I could carry him in the back or in the front. Black berries were ripe as was the mountain huckleberries. Me and my baby picked berries til they were all gone. My baby was such a good boy, he would make goo goo sounds while I would sing an old hymn as I would pick the berries, he was a good baby Mac. I saved all of my berry money and I hid it all. The berry patches were all picked out and me and my baby went out for walks. One night I heard Mom and Vanna talking and I heard Mom say he's a good looking baby and he will sell for a good price. Vanna said Mom how much should we ask for him? Mom said no less than a thousand dollars. Vanna said Joe may get more for my baby. Mom said anyway it goes he leaves here in the morning. I knew who the he was and no way would they sell my baby. I was on the highway the next day early with my baby. I had took my clothes and his and I was hitchhiking, my baby seemed to enjoy leaving the place behind us. I didn't know or care where we were going. I had very little money from picking berries but your Mom and Dad said God would make a way and provide for me and I believe what God said. So here I am going somewhere with my baby. A car stopped and a man rolled the car window down. He said Ma'am I know you need a ride, I hope you don't mind to ride in the back seat. I've got the front seat full of my papers. I didn't mind riding in the back seat and he was a nice man. My baby slept all of the ride which was a long ride. We talked a lot about his family and how it cost so much to raise up a child. He stopped and said Ma'am I've went past where I was to stop. I wanted to get you out of town so you may get a ride. I got out of his car and he said Ma'am let me shake your hand. I reached my hand out and he took my hand and said there's a good town ahead of you. He moved his hand and here I held a bill, a fifty dollar bill. I said why Mister do this? He said it's the least I can do for you and your baby. He said some day you may help someone in need, now you will take care of your baby, but take care of yourself too. I said I love you Mister and I cried, oh the love I felt for this nice man. I walked on carrying my baby in the front as I cried. My baby looked up at me and he seemed to ask, Mom why are you crying, you have me. yes I had my precious baby, the only thing that would ever matter to me. I came to a small cafe and I went in to eat and take care of my baby. I ordered a small meal to make it all look good. I ate and a waitress asked if there was anything else I wanted. Yes Ma'am I need to change my baby and wash him off. Come on she said and she showed me to the restroom. Go ahead and do what you need to do, I'll stay at the door, you wash yourself if you want. I felt like I had better wash myself for I didn't know what lie ahead. I took care of our wash off and the girl said what about the baby, do you give him your titty? Oh no I said he's on the formula and I need to fix him a bottle or two. She said our cook will help you do that as I watch. Oh he's a Dad so he knows what to do. My baby's formula was ready and I said goodbye too all the nice people. I passed by the cashier and she said didn't you forget something? Oh I'm sorry I forgot to pay for my food. A waitress said no not that, here she said as she came to me with her handful of bills. She said it's our tip money, the cook put in ten bucks and you need it worse than we do. I looked at all the bills she had gave me and wanted to cry. She hugged my neck and said I know you will take care of your baby but you take care of yourself for him. I felt as if I was going to cry, so I began to hug each one of them, yes the cook too. I said I'll never be able to repay you for all you have done for me. The cook said that is right but there may come the day in your life that you can help someone in need. Now he said when you help that person you will pay us back with a dividend. I will never forget what that group told me as I left. They all said go with God speed, I did cry then for sure. I loved those people and I loved that town. I spent the rest of the day trying to find a place that I could work and keep my baby with me. The day passed and no work did I find for me and my baby. I had to get a motel room for me and my baby. We took our first bath in a bathtub that night. Oh me and my baby had fun in that big tub. We had a tub fill of bubbles and we played for over an hour in the tub. I had my baby pulled up between my legs as he splashed the water and laughed. I had so much love for my baby that I could cry. I wondered why all people couldn't be like the man that gave me my first ride and all the nice people at the cafe. I tried to find work but none did I find where I could keep my baby. My baby and I ended up in a homeless shelter for a place to sleep and eat. The people that ran the place was nice but the man told me he couldn't let me stay there forever, that I would have to move on in two days. I didn't know what to do but I knew God would make a way for me and my baby. That night I prayed for God to show me the way I was to go the next day. Before I was to leave the shelter a lady passed by me and my baby and she stopped and said dear what are you and your baby doing here? She sat down and played with my baby as I told her all I dared to tell her at the time. So you want a job where you will be near your baby. Well get what you have here and let's go. Soon me and my baby had us a job as a housekeeper and cook in this nice lady's home, well more cook than anything else. Her name was Laureen Hammonds and her husband was Harvey. They became the Mom and Dad I never had, they gave me love. My baby became their Grandson, oh they never had any children, no other family at all. Oh me and my baby loved our new Mom and Dad. Mom asked when was the baby's shots due. I told her that I hadn't took him in for his shots. Mom said he has to go as soon as we can get him in for his shots. Mom said you will need his birth certificate. I dug out his papers and handed them to Mom. Hannah why don't he have a first name, I looked and I saw a no name Douglas on the paper. Mom said all baby's deserve a name, so name your baby. I said Mom I don't know what to name my baby but I want a real strong name for him. Mom said before you go to sleep tonight read first Samuel chapter one and see if the story leads you in any way. Yes I read the chapter and it did fit me. Hannah couldn't conceive and her hand maiden bare a child for her, so Vanna bared my baby for me and I knew it was God's will that I had my baby to care for and his name is Samuel MacDouglas.

Time passed and I remember one year I had got a virus and Mom made me stay in bed. One evening as I lay in bed I heard a knock at my door, it was Harvey and I told him to come in. He came in with a tray of food and sat it down on the bedside table. I had both hands under the sheet and he ran his hand under the sheet. I thought oh God not him to, like my Dad. He pulled my hand from under the sheet as I lay with my eyes closed waiting for him to do what my birth Dad had done to me when I was young. I felt a damp feel on my hand and I opened my eyes. Dad had a wet wash rag and he was wiping each of my fingers in such a gentle loving way, he then washed my other hand the same way then he turned the wash rag over and washed my brow and my face. He said now get yourself up in the bed, you have to eat and get well, we love you. I had never felt so much love as this before, and he kissed my brow. I began to stop my hate for Dad and

Mom and Vanna, yes you to but I couldn't hate the man I love as the others. At this time I began to feel a love that I had never known and I felt it from the nice man who gave me a ride and all the nice people at the cafe and to my new Mom and Dad. I wanted to be independent so Mom helped me, I had a job in a day care and saved all I could. Mom and Dad helped me to get a small house and get it set up, then Mom kicked my ass out. Oh she was at my house every day or I was at hers. Harvey was a Dad to Mac, as he was called. He was at ball games or even there to take Mac fishing. Harvey and Lauren put Mac through college and Harvey put Mac to work for him after college. Mac began to take over Harvey's company as Harvey wished. Then my dear Dad passed on leaving all he had to Mom. All the years after I left the homeless shelter me and Mom went back to the shelter. We helped all of those we could help, there were so many needing help that we couldn't help them all, we helped all we could. It hurt Mom that she couldn't help all of the people that were in need. Some only got words from us but that's all that some needed at the time. Mom said to me one day, Hanna don't you think Samuel should know who his Father is? Yes don't you think the father should know he has a Son. Now Mom said call this man and tell him all you can about Samuel's father. So I called a PI and gave him what I wanted to know and I wanted to be sure. He took some time but he got what I wanted and it was all good. Now my dear loving Mon passed on before we got the PI's report. Now Mom left me all she owned, the business and all assets. So Mister Arthur "Mac" Douglas I don't need or want your money, all I ever wanted from you was your love and for you to take me with you when you left me crying. Oh I'm glad it has turned out as it has. It has been God's will to give me my baby to care for and for me to get it after the hate I had for so many people. I'm glad it has turned out like it has for my baby's sake and for my baby to grow up with so much love. Some years back Mom and I did a search for Vanna and we learned a lot through court records. Yes Joe Peters and Vanna and Mom were all tried and all found guilty of trying to sell a baby. Well first Joe and Vanna got married and she gave birth to another baby. Now I knew before I left that my Dad had screwed Joe's Mom. Joe's Dad had screwed my Mom and Joe and Vanna were Brother and Sister. Anyway they all needed money so Joe and Vanna kidnapped a baby right before store cameras and Mom helped in the whole deal. They were set up to sell the baby in a parking lot, the buyers were FBI agents. Joe and Vanna got a thirty year sentence and Mom got fifteen years. Vanna died of rectal cancer, Joe died of lung cancer and Mom, she just died, I guess from being mean. Well I don't or didn't have any family and it didn't matter, I had my baby. Now Samuel is married to a most lovely girl, her name is Carol and her family has wealth but she's not a stuck up. We go to the homeless shelter at least once each week to help all we can. Oh yes you are going to be a Grandpa soon. Now I'm going to see our Son and it's your choice of what you do and Samuel doesn't know about all of this. Now whatever you decide I will always love you as much as I did as I begged you to take me with you. Yes Vanna said when you first screwed her that you tore her pussy apart. Now Mac I've only seen Dad's little one in a dark room and I wouldn't know how big a dick is to be. Now if I were to take your dick in my pussy that's never had a dick would you tear my pussy apart? Mac reached in and gave Hanna a long kiss, then said Hannah I haven't ever hurt any woman as Vanna may have said. She said Mac why did you kiss me? Mac said because it's what I've wanted to do since we were young kids. Hannah said here Mac is what I wanted to do since I was a young girl. She gave him a kiss that she had wanted to give him for many years. Mac said let's go see our Son. She said Mac, Samuel doesn't know one thing about what Mom and I have done. The DNA is to be a positive test for Samuel to be your birth Son, please feel free to get your own DNA test done. Mac if you meet Samuel and there is a doubt by you then you get your own test done done. Please whatever you do don't hurt my Son. I've took care of my baby along with my Mom's help and I won't have him hurt. So if you do meet your Son and if you have any doubt in your heart about being his Father just walk away and don't hurt my baby please. I won't beg you to take me with you again. Mac said why did you wait so long to do all of this? Hannah said Mac you have never had the joy of raising a child and you wouldn't know all of this.

Now Mac I loved my baby but it hasn't been all a big bed of roses. You haven't seen the need to stay up all night with a sick baby when you were so tired and sleepy you didn't know how you were going to to make it that day. No you missed all of that and then turn the baby over to Mom as you went to work, then sleep a few hours that night and then do it all over again. When I left home with my baby I vowed I would always take care of my baby. I couldn't have done what I did if I hadn't had a loving Mom and Dad to help me. We all raised a Son that we were proud of. I wanted to raise my Son up in a way that your Mom and Dad would be proud of. Oh yes Samuel is a Deacon in a Baptist church and Carol and I teach a Sunday school class. Hannah said Mac I haven't been kissed before and when you kissed my lips something happened like I never thought about. Mac I'm dumb about men and woman things but now why did my pussy get hot and wet from your kiss. Mac said if you did I suppose it's because that's what you were wanting if you have never done the such. Mac could this lead me to wanting more than just a kiss from you? Yes he said it could lead to wanting to do more. She said you want to try me and see how much I may want after a few of your kisses? Yes he said we can if you want to and think it's safe. Oh she said let's try a few more kisses as we wait for our taxi. She said Mac now just why did your dick get so large all of a sudden? He said I would think it's because I've got the girl I left behind here in my arms. She said and your dick won't tear my pussy apart if it went in it? No he said let's kiss. Hannah said now Samuel knows all about Vanna and how she was and all that she did. Hannah said he's at home with Carol waiting for me but they don't know about you. Hannah said Mac how am I to tell them, or Samuel about his birth Father? Mac said oh let's go in and find out.

Samuel met them at the door with Carol. Samuel said well Mom I was wondering if you and Dad got lost. Hannah said now wait a minute you just called this man Dad. Samuel said Mom did you think you were the only person that could hire a PI and get a DNA test done. No Mom Dad was searching for me for years, and he found me. I didn't want to spoil it all for you so I didn't say anything. Mom I hope you aren't mad. Hannah hugged Samuel and said I have never been mad at my baby or Son. Samuel said Mom I've heard you since I was little cry for your one love and I knew one day your love would find you and well, Dad's here so let's eat. Carol said yes Mom let's go set the table while these two talk. Hannah said Carol did you know that Samuel and his Dad had already met? Yes Mom we all knew but you had worked so hard to get Samuel and his Dad together. None of us could spoil this for you, I hope you're not mad. Hannah hugged Carol and said you will be a great Mom. Carol said Mom Samuel and I want you to enjoy the rest of your life, and Samuel has heard you cry for his Dad's love since he was born, so you need to go after his Dad. Heck Carol said you are young and lovely and got a fresh one I would guess, so get what you have wanted for so long. Hannah said but what I've wanted I've been afraid he would tear my pussy apart. Carol said look at me, and Samuel is a large man and my pussy isn't tore apart. Samuel's Dad won't hurt your little girl's pussy, so get him in it. After some months of courting Hannah and Arthur "Mac" Douglas were wed. Hannah got her first one in her pussy on her wedding night. She knew one thing and that was she loved the feel of his large one up in her pussy. She didn't know her pussy would ever receive or give so much pleasure. She thinks of all the berries she and her baby picked to get away from the past that had no future for them. She never thought that making love with her only love could ever be as perfect to her as it is. She knew it would be filled with love, but not so perfect. She still does all the charity work that she can. Now she's got a Grandson to help Carol with and to help spoil. She thinks at times about all of the things that Vanna did and she knows that Vanna's life was ruined by her Dad. Hannah feels bad for Vanna and she loves her. Hannah life isn't perfect but close to it.

The End of
Take Me With You

Like Daughter, Like Mother

Ken caught a cab and got a ride to his barber across town. Bob his barber for several years was closed when he got to the shop. When he had got to the shop the last time he got there late in the evening. Ken got to the shop only to find the door locked. He wondered why Bob would close his shop so early in the day. Ken read from a piece of paper taped on the inside of the door glass, for service call this phone number. Ken called the number from his cel phone, mostly to try to find out why Bob would be closed so early. A woman answered and said please don't leave if you are calling about service, I'll be right down. Ken wondered who had answered the phone and how and what did she have to do with Bob's barber shop. Ken looked up at the sky and it looked like it would be another rainy weekend in the city. He couldn't recall when he had seen the sun shine or even a star shine. A young woman said are you the man that called for service? Ken looked at a very lovely well built young woman and said I called but who are you? Mister I'm here to give you service, now come on in the shop please. Yes that's it just get up in the barber chair and I'll take care of you. He heard some noise behind him and the shop got dim. Oh my I forgot to turn on the lights, now that's better, at least you may see me now. She said close your eyes for I have to do this. He heard running water then a cold rag was placed over his eyes. What is this he asked, I just wanted a hair cut, that you will get but for now I've got to get you ready. Now let me loosen you up as I do this as she began to massage his neck and shoulders. Now doesn't that feel good Mister, I know you love it don't you? He said yes that's nice but why do that? For this she said as she pushed the barber chair around. Mister when you get your tongue back in your mouth tell me how you like them. Ken's mouth was the closest that it had been to a woman's breast in many years. Mister I can let you look at them but I don't think it's legal for you to touch them. I bet you would love to touch them wouldn't you? Oh I had better let the barber in before the door gets knocked down. I'm coming she yelled out, don't beat the door down. She opened the door and in walked another girl that could have been the other girl's Sister. I hope I've got him ready for you barber. Ken said you are the barber, where's Bob? She said Mister how do you want it, I do mean the hair cut? Ma'am Ken said can you just give me a trim if you know how to cut hair. She said I have a barber's license for this city, oh yes for the whole state, now how about that Mister? He said give me a trim but no shave. Here let me do this and maybe you will stop shaking so bad, then maybe you won't. She said Mister do you like mine, oh I knew you would but don't touch them please. Ken was looking at two pair of lovely titty's as the girls stood before him. Mister put your tongue back in your mouth, I don't want to get hair on it, well not your hair. Ken sat in the barber chair the longest he could remember since his Mother held him in the barber chair for his first hair cut so long ago. Mister what do you think about it. Ken never looked in the mirror as he said that's all right. She said then it's not the way you want it is it, I can take more off but I can't put any back on. Ken said the hair cut is fine, the service is fine but why all the service as you say? Mister you have my number and if you give me your number and address we will give you the rest of the service. He said are you sure you would do that? Yes Sir we would do that. Yes Sir we would if you don't live out of the state. Ken wrote his address on a piece of paper then gave it to the girl. She looked at the other girl and said what time do we get there? Ken said you said we, who do you mean as we? She will be with me we are a team and we come as a package deal you can say. Ken said is seven pm tonight alright? The first girl said MIster any time is alright, we will be there. Ken said that was a good hair cut and I'll be back, bye now. Hey Mister the hair cut is cheap but not free. Oh yes he said as he give the girls some bills. The girls looked at the money in their hands as he went out the door. Bye they said as he got in his cab, we will see you tonight. It was a real down pour by the time he got in the front of his building. He took a shower and looked for the first time at the hair cut. It was a nice hair cut the girl had gave him and he had forgot to ask about Bob and where he was. He ate his meal and did some paper work and took a pee then turned on the TV to the weather channel. It was going to be another long wet weekend. He lay in bed and thought about the lovely girls at the barber shop. They could pass for twins but one seemed to be more of a pusher than the other. Ken went through the TV channels and as many channels that he had there wasn't anything that he wanted to watch. He laughed about the girls being to see him at seven pm. Now it was past eight pm and the girls most likely were having a good time with his money.. He turned his TV off and was ready to go to sleep. Ken was awakened by someone pounding on his door. he went to see who would be at his door this late. He peeped through the door peep hole, there he saw a young girl. He opened the door and said I see that you got wet. May we come in Mister, please we are soaked and our clothes are soaked. Yes come in he said and they both tried to walk through the doorway at the same time. One girl stepped back and said you go first this was all your big idea. Now the other girl said it was our idea and you go in first, no you go first, no you go first, no you go first. Ken said girls come in and get out of your wet clothes. They looked at each other and one of the girls said see I told you that he would. Mister where's your bathroom where we can get out of our wet clothes. He said it's in here, do you need any help with your clothes? No you get ready for us and we will he ready soon. Ken went back to bed and he would let them take care of their soaked clothes. Mister we are ready and I'll tell you now we aren't a flooky and you will use a rubber, yes and wash it before you put it on. He said do you mean for me to wash the condom or to wash it. Mister please don't make it harder. Oh my I said the wrong words I believe. Mister we have never done anything like this before, help us please. Ken said girls are you wearing anything under those towels? He looked at two lovely girls and these were real full all out all over girls. One girl said see I told you he wouldn't like us. Mister what's wrong with us that you don't like us? Girls he said both of you are cold and shivering, now get in the bed. Mister are you going to screw us both in one night? He said girls let's get some blood back in circulation in your lovely body's for now, come on in or I'll get up and let you have my bed. It would help if I lay in the bed with you. Alright let's get in the bed with him I don't think he wants to screw us anyway, I've heard of men that couldn't do it. I guess he's one of them. One girl said you go first, no you go first, no you go first, then one said get set, get ready, on the count of three, one, two, three and he had both girls in bed with him. Mister we are shaking I guess but it's not from the cold rain, heck we are so excited we could just pee couldn't we, yes the other girl said. Ken said girls get settled down and here let me put my arms around you, yes that's it just snuggle up against me real close if you girls want to. One girl said I know I'm gong to like you, me too the other girl said. He lay and held the girls til they stopped shivering then he heard it, let's do it and they kissed him at the same time. One girl said get the rubber on I wlll go first, that's what we decided to do. Why a rubber he said aren't you on birth control? Oh we are on birth control but it don't keep you from getting a disease. He said and you may give me a disease. No we are clean as a pin one girl said. He said you said it was to keep me from getting a disease. Mister I don't know what I said but our pussy's are clean and I'll swear for both of us. I bet you don't even have any rubbers do you? He said girls I have never needed a rubber before and no I don't have any rubbers. You should have got some I told you we would be here. Yes I do believe you said at seven pm didn't you. Yes Mister we did and I'm sorry we were late. Ken said girls I'm going to take a pee, no don't get up I will get over top of the one next to the bathroom. He went to the bathroom and in the floor lay the girls wet clothes all but their panty's. Their panty's they had left on top of the commode tank. He hung up the girl's clothes after he had wrung the water out of them. He picked up a pair of pretty red panty's and they were dry except for a damp place in the crotch. Both girls had wore near the same pantry color and each one was wet in the same place. Ken got a whiff of a heavenly aroma from each one of the girl's panty's. He held each pair to his face and thought of how long it had been. Mister, Mister does it take you this long to take a pee? He went back to the bed and one girl said well do you like what you see? Ken looked down at the girls with their legs spread apart. He got back in bed between the two girls and lay down. One girl said Mister tell us what to do for you to get you to screw us. Yes the other one said Mister neither of us have ever done the such as this but we learn fast, please. Oh the other girl said I told you back at the shop that we couldn't give our pussy's away. Yes the other one said you are right let's get dressed and go home. Okay on the count of three one, two, three. Wait Ken said you can't leave yet. Then you are going to screw us? No he said, girls your clothes that you both left in the bathroom on the floor that I wrung out and hung up, they are still soaking wet. Mister we are sorry but we came to please at least one man in this city, and we are sorry about our wet clothes. The other girl said let's just wear our wet clothes and go home. I told you no one would want our pussy's here in this town. He said girls you can't go home in your wet clothes as they are. You mean you want us to stay and you will screw us? That's not the way I meant it, girls not one cab driver in this city would let you in his cab in those wet clothes. So that's it and you don't want to screw us, I bet you can't even get him hard, that's it you have got a dead dick. Oh I'm sorry I didn't mean to say all of that. He said now why do you want me to screw you as you say? One girl said the why at the start was about another matter that I won't talk about for now. Mister if we were one of them flooky girls now would you, I mean could you screw one of those girls? Girls I'm not sure of what you mean but if I ever do make love I hope for it to be with a lovely girl like you both are. Mister if you do screw us who would be screwing us, if you even could get him hard. Girls my name is Ken and I don't believe I heard your names. Ken I'm Renae and she's my older Sister Zenae, now will you screw us please, that is if you can. Ken said I can't because you said I would have to use a rubber and I haven't used a rubber in many years. The girls looked at each other and Renae said let's screw him Zenae, he's a clean good looking man. Zenae said you go first because this was mostly your big ideal. Renae said no Zenae I've been screwed three times, or barely screwed three times. Zenae, you said you have been screwed two times so you get screwed first. No Zenae said you go first. Renae said no let's do it like we have always done it. Okay here we go, one, two, three. Renae said Zenae you always win, now go get Ken's dick in your pussy. Yes Zenae I will watch as Ken screws your pussy as you can watch him screw mine. Ken said girls don't I have a say in this? Renae said yes you can say all you want but it won't matter. He said Zenae is your pussy wet now? Ken my pussy has been sort of wet since I first saw you back at the shop. Ken said we better go wash it before we start. Zenae said before we start? Renae said mine's wet too, do I wash my pussy too? Ken said let's go girls I'll wash both of you girls pussy. Zenae said Renae I didn't know about this, now what do we do? Renae said we let Ken wash our pussy's, so let's go, I can't wait for this. Ken she said can we wash your dick? He said my dick's not wet. No Zenae said but may we wash it anyway? He said girls let's go and get your pussy's ready to screw for now. Yes Renae said let's get this washing pussy thing over with so we can get our pussy's screwed. My Ken our clothes won't get dry tonight will they? Ken washed the girl's pussy's as they giggled like young school girls. Ken, Renae said my pussy has been dry for some time. Zenae said yes mine is dried to Ken so let's go to bed. In the bed he said girls are you sure of this? Yes they both said. Zenae said I'll be pleased if I can feel your dick in my pussy, so do all you want to do. Ken said you both can still back out and lay in bed til your clothes get dry. Zenae said Ken give me and my pussy all you can. Renae said yes and don't forget my pussy Ken. Ken said if you want to stop at any time just say stop or don't and I will and we stop but I won't ever start back with you. Renae said Ken just screw Zenae's pussy all you can then get your dick up in my pussy, that is if you can. Ken said are you really sure you want to do this? Yes, yes and double yes they said. Now get to screwing when you can, that is if you can. Ken started on top kissing his way down to her large titty's. Zenae began to moan as he sucked each one, then he was between her legs and he could smell her heavenly aroma from her pussy and feel the heat. Zenae went wild when he got his tongue on her large clit. She said if your dick's hard my pussy wants your dick, like now. Ken got his dick near her wet pussy and said if you want my dick put him in your pussy. Oh Ken you mean I get to do it, yes and here he goes in my pussy. Ken I've never screwed before so tell me how can I please you. He said do as you feel like doing. Zenae's pussy came alive and she sure could work her pussy as Ken gave her his dick. Ken was ready and so was she. He shot her pussy full as she screamed as she shot off as he kept on screwing her pussy as she yelled and screamed. Zenae stopped screaming and Renae said did Ken hurt your pussy Zenae, you were screaming. Zenae said no Ken wasn't hurting my pussy and really was I screaming? Yes Renae said you were screaming and really loud. Zenae said Renae I've never thought a dick would make me scream. Renae said Sis if Ken gets hard again you can screw him all he can. Zenae said no Sis I want to watch Ken screw your pussy and see if you scream. Zenae said Sis I believe Ken may have a large dick so get your pussy ready for his large dick. Renae said Ken we haven't screwed before so when you get ready I will be ready for your dick. Ken said I had better go wash my dick off before I screw your pussy Renae. Oh no Ken she said this is the main thing we want to do, we are Sisters and my pussy is the same as hers and so is our juices, so I'm ready. Ken said here we go if you are ready. I'm ready Renae said but are you ready, I mean is your dick hard? Ken gave her the same as he gave Zenae but this girl was the hot one. She went wild when he sucked her titty's and he sucked them for a while and she moaned. Renae said Ken my pussy is ready and I'm ready so put your dick in my pussy when you are ready. Oh yes I want it to last for a long long time, a really long time. Ken moved to her hot wet pussy with his mouth and tongue as she moaned. Her clit was large like Zenae's and she was wild now, put him in my pussy any time Ken. He said you want my dick you put him in. She wasted no time and soon she was getting her pussy screwed. She went wild as he screwed her pussy hard as she pushed her pussy up to him. Ken shot her pussy full as she shot off and screamed as he shot her pussy full again.

Ken lay between the girls and ran his hands over their lovely bodies. Zenae said Ken was our pussy's good for you? I mean did our pussy's please you, did you like our pussy's? Ken said girls you both have good pussy's, yes your pussy's pleased me. I just love you girls and I love and also like your pussy's Renae said see Zenae I told you Ken would be pleased with our pussy's. Zenae said Ken you gave me my first pleasure that I've ever felt from my pussy, it was so good when I felt you shoot my pussy full, I felt like I was ready to scream. Renae said Ken I couldn't have said it any better, and I was filled with such a pleasure I had never felt before, I wanted to scream too. Ken said girls were you really pleased with all I tried to do for you, yes you both did scream, and loud too. Zenae said Ken if you were to get a hard dick my pussy is hot and I want your dick back up in my pussy.

Renae said yes and if you can will you please screw my pussy before, well please do what you can for us, Sis gets your dick first. Ken hugged the girls up close to him and Zenae said he's hard Ken so screw my pussy please. Ken gave the girls what they wanted and must have needed and they screamed. He lay between the girls and thought how they were so easy to please. Renae broke into his thoughts and said Ken I asked if you were married. No Renae I'm not married but I was for a time, now girls let's go get our shower and get ready for the day. Zenae said the day, now I'm not looking forward to this day. Ken said girls in life we each have to look at each day as a new beginning, a new opportunity for us each to do something that may be a help to each of us but first we should use each day to help someone else and feel good when we can help them. Zenae said Renae this man is a very smart and wise man. Yes Renae said he is and Ken what you said was very well said. You ready to wash our pussy's now Zenae said. Ken said get your lovely asses out of the bed and let's face the day. Both girls got something in the shower they hadn't dreamed of. Renae watched as Ken eased his dick up in Zenae's pussy from behind and Zenae pushed her hot pussy on his dick. Zenae said oh my Sis you will have to get you one of these, hold me up Sis. Zenae screamed loudly as she shot off. Renae said if you can screw my pussy Ken I'm ready. Renae was more than ready and she went wild with her pussy and she could work her pussy and her ass like wild. Ken shot her pussy full as she slipped out of Zenae and Ken's hands and fell down in the tub. Zenae said Sis get your ass up we have a lot to do if you have forgot. Ken got them all dried and their clothes were ready for wear. Ken said now girls I dress each of you. Sure Zenae said if you want to and get me first if you will.

He dressed Zenae and left her panty's laying on the bed til he got both of them dressed, then he held a pair of panty's to his face and inhaled the heavenly aroma then layed them down and inhaled the aroma from the other pair and lay them on the bed. Renae said now which one had the best smell, mine or Zenae's. Ken said pick up your panty's Renae. Oh Ken our panty's are alike and I don't know which panty I wore. Ken said as it is with your heavenly aroma you have the same heavenly aroma. The girls stood side by side and Ken pushed up their skirts and began to work their clits, he wanted to get them both to come together, that didn't take long before they both screamed. Zenae said you have made me and my pussy feel so good and I know Sis feels the same way. Renae said Sis I need to speak alone with Ken, let's go to your bathroom. Renae closed the bathroom door and faced Ken. She said you have done it to my Sis I guess you know. What do you mean he said. Renae reached in and pulled ken's lips to her for a long kiss. She turned Ken's lips loose and said you have made my Sis happy and I've never seen her this open in all my life, well I've known her all my life. I love you for all you have done for me and my Sis and I'll love you till I die. Ken I guess you think that me and Sis are some sort of bad girls don't you? Ken this is the first and the wildest thing we have ever done. Again, thanks Ken for giving us our pleasure with your love, I hope we have pleased you and your dick too. Zenae was at the door and she yelled Renae are you screwing Ken, I want to get screwed again if you are. Renae said we are coming out, I got something in my eye and Ken helped to get it out. Zenae said Sis you know that neither one of us could lie and you were the worst liar that got our ass spanked at home. Zenae said Sis we have a lot we have to talk about and what we can do and it's a long way home. Renae said yes Ken we better kiss you bye and head for home. Ken said girls do you think you can just walk in my room in your rain soaked clothes and get screwed and just walk away from me? Zenae said Ken you are right and we will screw you all day if you want, that is if you can get hard, won't we Sis. Yes Renae said I'm ready Ken. Ken said girls I had it in my mind to go out for a good breakfast for my girls. Zenae said I can eat but I would rather let you screw my pussy. Renae said Ken we will do whatever you want, I believe my hot Sis is letting her little pussy take over her mind. Zenae said Sis you do know this will be our last chance to get our pussy's screwed with Ken's good dick don't you. Ken said girls let's go eat and then see how you both feel. Zenae said Ken now speaking of feel do you want to feel me up again? No Renae said Sis he doesn't, now get your little hot ass out the door, come on Ken and lock your door. Ken got the girls settled at a table in a nice little eating place near where he lived. Both girls ate as if they were starved. Zenae said Ken have you ever screwed a girl on a table in a place like this? Ken I'm ready now to let you screw my pussy right here and now. Renae said Sis that won't happen here so forget it. Ken said Zenae I never have done as you just said but to make my girls happy I would screw you on a table, not here though. Renae said Sis it's time to tell Ken about us so here I go. Ken Sis and I have good parents and they gave us what they could. They pushed us to study and learn, Mom was the main pusher. Zenae got her cherry popped and that was it. A year later I got mine popped, Sis got a dick in her pussy in our last year of high school. I had got me a dick the year before. I got me another one in college. We never got any pleasure and we knew we should have. My pussy I guess was hotter then Sis was, I wanted me a good dick but I didn't get one. Before college was over after six years we began to send out resumes so sure we could take our pick of any place to work. we went home with our degrees running out of our asses. we helped Mom clean a clean house for a while, then we got lazy assed and all we did was watch TV and lay around and eat, we were slobs I know. One morning Mom pulled our asses out of bed and it wasn't morning, it was afternoon. Mom lowered the boom on us. She said girls you both are so much better than to lay on your asses and do nothing, I'm putting both of you out of the nest. Mom layed it all on the line for us, she was going to kick us out and we couldn't get back in til we were successful. We had to do our own dirty clothes which our Mom had just let pile up in the laundry room. The wash had gave us more time at home. During our wash cycles Mom got a phone call and talked for a while and then said yes I will. Mom had never looked as she was at the time, she looked sick. I ran to her and asked her what was wrong that she looked so pale? Zenae came back to us with a wet wash cloth and began to wipe Mom's face and brow. I said Mom what's wrong, was it a pervert phone call? Mom said girls the call was about your Uncle Bob. I said but Mom we don't have an Uncle Bob. Yes Uncle Bob was her Brother. He went to a barber school and got his license and said he was going to the big city. Uncle Bob just got lost from all of his family and I guess he was just forgot about til Mom got the phone call. I said Mom it was good that he called after all these years. Ken it wasn't Bob it was his attorney. Uncle Bob died and left the barber shop and all of his assets to Mom. Yes he had been cremated, no funeral, no nothing, that gave Sis and I a little more time to lay on our ass as the shock wore off of Mom. Mom made several phone calls over the next few days, then she slammed it to both of us right in our faces and I mean Mom knew how to hit really hard. She sure could be mean to her girls. Soon Mom had our sorry little asses in a Barber and hair salon school up to our asses. Zenae got her license, I didn't but that didn't slow Mom's ass down. Ken Mom kicked our sorry asses out to this city to take over Uncle Bob's barber shop. Heck we owned the shop and and got all of Bob's assets, now wasn't that real nice of our Mom. Oh my we were going to service all of this city we thought. Sis got a few I guess from other shops that they couldn't service. Ken to make it plain we have lost our asses in this city and we aren't successful so we can't go home. We had sent out our resumes all the while with no reply's. I don't guess our resumes were what they wanted as they all were, we had to hand write them. Ken what we pulled here last night isn't what we are. Sis and I made a plan of what we would do but I didn't expect it to go this far but I'm glad it did. Sis and I agreed that if either one met a man that we feel a love for we would give our hearts and our whole beings to the man. Ken we didn't know it would get this far and we aren't flooky's. Ken after you left the shop we hugged each other and put our tops on and ran to our landlord. Yes we have been evicted and dumb ass me I thought we could keep our room by paying part of our rent that was behind. He took our money then said the eviction stayed as it was. We had kept just enough of your money for a taxi to your place. I messed up on that and went to the wrong street. The ink smeared on the paper and I went to fifty eight street instead of fifty third street. Now here we are walking in a down pour and no money. Ken we messed up on your room number. Zenae said that was my fault. No Renae said it was our fault. Ken there's a lot of doors to knock on at your place and we split up on each floor and knocked from left to right. I guess we broke up some screwing in some of the rooms. I know we were late but we had sold our wrist watches two weeks before for food. This is the first we have ate in three days. Ken we can't go home so we have til Monday hen we go to a homeless shelter if we can get in. Zenae began to cry and Renae hugged her and said Sis please don't cry we will make it some way. Ken that's it and we gave you all we had to give to the best man in this city or world, that's the way it is. I won't let my Sis down, I will take care of her and love her. Ken said won't your Mom help you girls? Zenae said she most surely would if she knew how it was here but we won't let her know that her girls are failures. Ken said my girls will never be failures and don't think that you are. He said girls would you both move in with me until you can do better? Zenae said can I talk with my Sis alone for a few minutes? Sure Ken said I'm going to the restroom to wash my hands, my girls can talk all they want. Ken took a long bathroom break and payed for their meal and the girls were still talking so he looked at the old pictures on the restaurant walls. He felt a bump to his arm and Renae said let's sit down Ken and talk. Now Ken you would want to screw our pussy's if we moved in with you. Ken said sure I would but that's a woman's choice of who and when she gets screwed. Zenae said and it would be our choice? Yes Ken said. Zenae said Renae now I'm sure I love Ken. Yes Renae said and I love you Ken and we will move in with you, temporally now. Zenae said Ken I know you are the best man in this city. Renae said and the luckiest also because our periods are at different times, so you can have all the best fresh young pussy you want at any time. Zenae said Ken we don't know about screwing so don't let us wear your dick out with our young pussy's.

We aren't all dumb and we know we are younger than you but I bet you can out screw any man in this city. Renae said Ken don't think of us being flooky's please. Ken said girls I believe that you mean floozies and that you will never be. Now my girls let's go pack your panty's. Zenae said Ken just about all we have are packed and ready for us to go to the homeless shelter. Zenae said Sis I've got an idea and here's what we will do as she whispered in Renae's ear. Renae said Sis let's go pee and get on the move to our place. Zenae said my pussy's getting hotter. Sis mine has been hot for Ken's dick since we left his place Renae said. The girls screwed Ken at their place in the bed, on the couch, in the bathroom or wherever they could for most of the day. Renae locked up the place and took the key to the landlord. The girl's looked back at Bob's shop with the closed sign in the window not knowing what was next. One thing the girls had plenty of was panty's of every color and Ken said I'll empty two of my chest drawers for your panty's. Zenae said we keep our panty's and our clothes together, we are the same in size in every thing I guess. Ken gave the girls all they wanted that night and they loved Ken and his hard dick. He found that the girls did have degrees as they said, running out their asses. He went over all the degrees they both had on Sunday. Ken said girls I have to make a phone call and it's a private call so go out and take in some fresh air and sun if it's still shining. They were gone for over a half an hour and Ken fixed them a meal and had it on the table when they came back. He said girls I began to think you had ran out on me, you were gone for so long. Renae said we didn't know how long your call would take, besides you had all of our clothes but what we wear. Zenae said Ken we won't ever run out on you, will we Sis. No Renae said not without our clothes, just kidding Ken.

He said girl's let eat. Zenae said and our lover can cook and screw. Renae we are the luckiest girls alive. Renae said one thing our Mom did make good out of us were cooks. Zenae could cook a worn out shoe and it would taste good enough to eat. Ken said girls let's eat where I can clean up in here, I need to talk to both of you. Zenae and Renae ate a good home cooked meal, their first in some time. They all cleaned up the kitchen and took a shower. After their shower Ken had both girls beside him on the bed and said girls I need to talk to both of you. Ken Renae said let us talk first please. while Sis and I went out for some air and sun we talked. Ken the great lover that you are, I'm sure you must have a real lover in town. We won't keep you from your real love as much as we need and want your love so feel free to screw and love all you want. Ken had tears rolling down his cheeks. I didn't mean to make you cry Ken, what did I say to hurt you so much. Ken hugged the girls and said you two are my only loves now. Now girls I called a friend of mine after both of you went out. Here is the deal, I've got both of you set for an interview for a well established company in this city. Here's the address and don't smudge it. From all I've heard from my girls neither of you have been in a interview. This is it just be honest and don't be to pushy but show what you feel that you can do for his company. Tell what you have studied and know about his company. Don't ever lie about what you don't know just be honest. Now don't ever be a flirt in an interview, the day of showing a little of your panty's or skin don't work in today's world when there's open pussy and dick all around. You must get to the interview early and drain all the pee out of your bladder you can. An interviewer doesn't like a pee break every few minutes. If you really need to pee don't sit there and fidget and try to hold it in, ask if you may be excused but pick the right time, don't interrupt him for a pee break, now can you do that? Renae said there's one problem that I see, we don't know one thing about this company. Ken said if you want to take notes here's all you need. Now listen up for I won't have time to go over all of this again. Ken began to talk about the company as the girls listened to Ken. Both girls sat and listened to Ken talk about the company til midnight. My girls that's all we have time for, any questions? Zenae said yes Ken aren't we supposed to have a call back number if we are lucky enough to need to be called and we don't have a phone. Ken said oh just use our number here. Renae kissed Ken's lips and Zenae gave him a kiss. Zenae said Ken you said our number and now I feel like I'm at home. Yes Renae said I feel the same way, now will you screw our pussy's please. Ken gave the girls what they both wanted and they must have got wore down, they went to sleep. Ken woke the girls early for breakfast the next next morning. Renae said we will skip breakfast. Ken said you don't ever go to an interview without eating. He said now get your little asses on the move. We have to pee first Renae said. They ate and showered and the girls wanted a good luck screw in the shower and they both got what they wanted. Ken gave the girls money and went to his job. The girls had time to study their notes before their interviews, of course the girls had separate interviews and Renae went first. The girls did as Ken told them to do and left a call back number and went home to wait for a call. In the middle of that week after Ken had got home from work the girls got a late evening call. Each girl talked on the phone for a while and ran and kissed Ken. Renae said we got a position as Ken said but we have a problem Ken. Yes Zenae said we are to dress business like. Ken we don't have one thing that looks business like unless we were hookers wearing our hot panty's. Renae said Ken should I call the man and tell him we can't take the job. Ken said girls I don't think you would start to work in the middle of week so just cool your little asses down. Ken said girls let's celebrate your new job. Renae said Ken get your dick in my hot pussy now. Zenae said get my pussy too Ken. Both girls got their pussy's screwed til after midnight. Zenae said Ken that was great for my pussy but it didn't make my short ass skirts any longer, not mine either Renae said. Ken said girls do you want to screw some more now or go to sleep? Zenae said Ken my pussy's ready for your dick any time now. Both girls got another good hot screwing and let Ken go to sleep. Zenae said in a whisper, Renae that was some good screwing but what about our work clothes? Zenae said let's go to sleep and let's do as Ken says, we will face a new day tomorrow. After they screwed and ate breakfast that Saturday morning Ken said girls let's go shower and then I'm taking my girls shopping for their work clothes. He said I hope you both know what you need to wear to work. He said I want my girls to get ten outfits complete, that's bras, panty's, shoes and all you will need. Zenae said Ken no man has ever bought anything for us before, do you think it's right for you to do that? Ken said girls get your little asses on the move, so we will have time to screw tonight. The girls looked at each other for a while and Renae said we have panty's we haven't wore. Zenae said my bras won't hold my titty's, you reckon it's because we have screwed our pussy's to much? Renae said I heard a girl in school say that screwing had made her titty's grow. What do you think Ken? He said girls let's just do your shopping, I don't know is my answer. Ken helped the girls all that he knew how but this was new to him. They couldn't believe the total when it was all checked out.

When they got home and put all of their purchases away Zenae said Ken did you pay for our clothes just to get to screw our pussy's? Ken turned and opened the door and said my girls fix and eat your meal I won't be eating, I'm not hungry. Yes girls I forgot it but I have work to do tonight, well and tomorrow also. I'll see you tomorrow night late I guess and he left. Zenae said reckon what Ken works at that he has to work on the weekend. Renae said I don't know but he's been acting sort of strange since we got our jobs. Zenae said let's do as he said for us to do. Renae said I'm afraid it's going to be a long ass weekend without Ken. Zenae said it's only been a week since we moved in with Ken, we barely know him. It was a lonely night and Sunday for the girls. Ken came home near midnight on Sunday and the girls were up waiting for him. Zenae said Ken we missed you and why were you so late getting home? Ken said girls go to bed you need to be on top of your new job tomorrow. Renae said Ken are you going to screw our pussy's for us tonight? Go to bed and go to sleep I'm going to take my shower, now go to bed. The girls went to bed and soon went to sleep. The girls had waited all the night before hoping that Ken would come home and screw their pussy's. The girls were awakened the next morning by the alarm clock. Renae said where's Ken, he's not in the bed. Zenae said I guess he went to work and if we don't move it we will be late for our first day at work. The girls rushed to get ready for their first day at work. The girls found a note and money Ken had left for them for food and cab fare. Yes girls I have some business I have to take care of out of town for a few days, so take care. The girls went to a whole new world and the girls went to work in different departments. The girls liked their job but where was Ken for so long? Ken came home late Friday night. Zenae said Ken we have missed you so much and you could have at least called us. Ken said girls just go on to bed and go to sleep and don't wait up for me. Renae said Ken don't you want to screw our pussy's? Ken said girls I hope that one day you may know that you each have more than your pussy's, now goodnight and go to sleep. The girls went to sleep and slept late on their first day off from work, but Zenae found Ken's note on the table that read, gone out don't wait up for me, Ken. Renae said Sis are we doing something wrong or would you know? Zenae said Sis I don't know but if we were doing something wrong as dumb as we are about matters as such as this we wouldn't know it. The girls spent a long boring weekend and they waited for Ken to come home. He came in after midnight to meet the girls at the door. Renae said me and Sis are dumb about some things but we can tell when we have went to far. Zenae said Ken we have done something wrong but we are to dumb to know what it is we have done. Renae said Ken you have been the closest thing we ever had for a boyfriend and yes we are dumb. Zenae said Ken we don't know how to fix a problem if we don't know what it is so tell us. Ken said girls you both need to learn that you have more to offer than a pussy. Now if I just wanted a pussy I can get all I want for free. Girls all I have done for you is to help you because I love you and not your pussy. Go to bed and go to sleep, I'm going to take a shower and go over some paper work, good night girls. Ken was gone to work the next morning when the girls woke up. We have done it again and Ken has done left for work I guess Renae said. When the girls got home from work that evening they found another note Ken had left for them, it said here's money for your cab fare and meals for the week, Ken. The girls sat down and cried because they were doing something that was bad wrong with Ken, but what? It was another long lonely week at home for the girls. Both girls were waiting for Ken when he came home late Saturday evening. Renae said Ken we know we have done or said something to hurt you but we don't know what it is unless you tell us. Zenae said Ken we both love you but not for all you have done to help us but because we love you. Ken said you have just answered your question but do you know the answer? Ken said girls when I saw you at your shop, yes I saw lovely women with lovely titty's, I saw more than your titty's and I felt a love for both of you and all I have done or will do for you will be done because I love the both of you and surely not just for your pussy's. Zenae said and you do really love us Ken? Yes girls as I said not just for your good hot pussy's. He said don't ever lower yourself down just for my dick or anyone's. Renae said Ken you will still screw our pussy's won't you? Ken said Girls as I have told both of you that will be your choice. Zenae said Ken this pussy, dick and screwing thing is all new to us and all we ever wanted to do was to please someone. Yes Renae said I don't know if we have pleased anyone before we met you, then we messed up with you. Ken said girls I'm going to take a shower. Renae said Ken my pussy and my love is all yours, now I've got you for all my own, Zenae is on her period. Zenae said I get his dick when your period starts ha, ha. Renae said my pussy is all yours and so is my love, now rush the shower, please. Renae got her good hard dick up in her that night. She said Ken please tell us when we do or say the wrong thing. Now it's hurt Zenae bad because we didn't know what to do to make it right. Ken said let's go to sleep my girls. Time passed and it was all smooth sailing at least for a while. The girls had the meal ready when

Ken got home. Renae said Ken let's eat, Sis and I need to have a talk with you. They ate and cleaned up the kitchen and Zenae said Ken if you want to take a pee you go on and take it. Ken said no let's get your talk over with. Zenae said we found out something about you that really disturbs me and Sis. Renae said Ken why didn't you tell us you were Kenneth Marshall, the CEO of your company and we worked for you. Yes Zenae said I found a picture I guess by mistake of you as the big man we worked for. Renae said Ken why didn't you tell us that we only got our jobs because we had gave you our pussy's. Yes we are really dumb to think we got our jobs on our own and not for our pussy's. Ken said girls the reason I didn't tell you is just what I'm hearing now from both of you. Girls I set both of you up for an interview but I never gave you your jobs or positions. Girls when will you learn that you are more than a pussy to me or my company. Girls sometime in this city a person can't get a job no matter what degrees that person has. Girls without a break a lot of good minds go to waste. The homeless shelters are full of lots of people with degrees but without a break they won't get anywhere. Girls as I have said before all I have done or will do is because I love both of you for who you are and not for the best pussy in this city or anywhere. Now is there anything else I can help my girls with? Yes Zenae said you can try to screw some sense into our heads, will you Ken? He said I don't think I can screw that long, I'll try. Ken said one more thing I don't tell my personnel director who to hire but do expect him to hire a person for the potential they have. He's not looking for pussy when he hires a female, he's a good family man with all girls and I can see now why he's bald headed at his age, his girls I guess. He said if no more I'm going to shower. Zenae said Ken please don't be mad at us for I told you we never knew how to act around men. Our Dad, we only saw on a Sunday then at times, he was to busy to talk to us. We never were interested in any man til you came into our lives and we just keep on messing up it seems. Ken said girls I love you and I'll always love you for you and not your pussy's. Ken my pussy is ready for your dick but I won't push you to take it but hurry up please. Ken and the girls got things ironed out, at least for some time. The girls were doing a good job and they both had been promoted in their departments. Ken asked the girls one evening if they had called their Mom recently? They looked at each other and Renae said no Ken we haven't talked to Mom and Dad since we were kicked out on our asses. We aren't a success yet as I see it so we can't go home and that's it. He said girls you need to call your Mom because she can't call you not knowing where you are. Renae said it's kind of like we don't know where you are every Friday night as it has been forever. He said girls you do have your Mom's phone number so you may cal l from here any time and at least let her know where you are and give her your number. Renae said Ken my pussy wants your dick so let's screw. Later Zenae said so Sis that's a homeless shelter. Yes Sis I guess it is but what's Ken doing here? Zenae said I don't know but let's go find out. Renae said no Sis let's not get to close he may see us and we have followed him all over the city to get this far. Renae said he's been inside the place for a long while, wonder what he's doing? Zenae said now how would I know what he's doing in there, he's been in there for a long while. Renae said Ken came out and look Sis at what Ken's doing. Renae said so that's it, he's buying his pussy here, look he's giving her some money and a paper. I bet it's his office number, Sis that's it. Ken has got tired of our pussy and he comes here to get it. Yes Sis I guess he's wore our pussy's out, now he's getting all he wants here, fresh pussy too. The girls faced Ken the next day about what they had seen him do at the homeless shelter. Zenae said why didn't you tell us that you were tired of our pussy's? Ken said girls will you tell me how many times that we screwed last night. Renae said yes we both got our pussy's filled three times last night and two each this morning. Ken said I don't believe I could take on another lover as hot as you girls are even if I was a young man. Renae said Ken we both saw you pay a woman and gave her a piece of paper, I bet it was your phone number. Ken said remember when I told you girls that in this city a degree didn't mean much without a break. Girls without a break where would you be now that you most likely wouldn't be here or in a shelter home. What you girls saw was a young lady as my girls were that needed a break. She will be in a room this weekend with clean clothes to be ready for a job interview Monday morning. No not with my company but a good company here in this city. Renae said but why did you help her? Ken said girls are you going to ever learn that it's easy to help someone if you have been in the same place that they are at this time. Ken said I'm going down to get some fresh air, it's sort of stagnated here with you two. Zenae said Sis our dumb asses have done it again. Renae said he could have just told us what he was up to. Sis Zenae said have you ever thought that we wouldn't have wanted all Ken did for us to be the front page news or even back page news. Some time in the evening Ken said girls I'll be taking a two week vacation and both of you are due a vacation. He said if you want you can take off as I will at the same time. Renae said do you mean for us to to spend our time with you? He said that's up to both of you about how you spend your vacation. Zenae said what beach do you go to Ken? Girls I have never been on any beach, I spend my vacation away from the beach. Zenae said we have never wore a bikini have we Sis. No Renae said and I won't wear one unless it's for Ken's eyes. Yes me to Sis Zenae said. Ken said you girls don't have to go anywhere, you can stay here and lay on your asses for two weeks. Where will you be going Ken? Girls I'll be going up state for a while as I usually do. The girls decided they would go with Ken wherever he would spend his vacation. They all were packed and Ken said I'm gone so be out front at the curb with your luggage waiting for me, oh yes you both take a long pee. The girls were at the curb as they were told by Ken when a car horn tooted, Ken rolled the car window down. Girls load up, oh don't forget your luggage. The girls loaded their luggage and got in the front seat with Ken. My Renae said Ken what a car, is it a rental? No Ken said it's mine. Zenae said Ken when did you buy the car? Ken said it's not a new car I've owned the car for several years. Renae said and you owned this car and we have rode a taxi's for years, why? Ken said one it's cheaper, two I don't like to fight all the traffic and all the lights and all the traffic tickets one will get in the city. Ken said I just hope you both did take a good long pee before you loaded up, oh did you all lock up our place? Yes Zenae said well I think we did. Aw Ken Renae said we were so exited to take our vacation with you. Zenae said I can remember when we were little girls and Dad and Mom would take us on a holiday drive as Dad called it. Mom and us girls would be busting to pee. Dad kept on driving because there were no places to pee. One time I guess it was on our last Sunday drive all of us girls needed to pee real bad. Dad pulled to a wide place and said girls there's the woods so go pee. Renae said we all jumped out of Dad's car and ran in the woods to pee. Mom needed to pee bad I guess because she was way ahead of me and Zenae. I saw Mom's bare ass squatting down taking her pee. I heard Zenae scream then I stopped then I saw it, the first wild animal I had ever seen, to make it short Zenae pissed all over herself as Mom just sat and laughed and squirted her pee. Zenae said Renae go ahead and tell the rest. Yes Ken that wild animal had scared the pee out of me and we both had wet our panty's, and pants. That big wild animal Mom later told us was a ground squirrel whatever that is. We later learned that it was the smallest wild animal in the woods. We drained out all the pee we could out of our pisser and got back in Dad's car wet as we were, that was the last of Dad's Sunday drives, it seemed that Dad put all of his time in his work after that day. Mom, she even changed after that day, we were used to a smile on her face and a glow but not after our last Sunday car ride. Renae said Ken the sign just read next stop restrooms, please we need to pee. Ken said girls we just got on the interstate and you were to drain your pissers before you left home. Zenae said we did but it must not have got all drained out, and I sure won't go back in any woods to pee. I won't either Renae said. Ken pulled up to the fuel pumps and said girls go pee while I fuel up the car. Ken said it's a long ways to the next restroom but there's some woods before we get there. Renae said this pee may take some time so you just wait or go get you a pee. Ken made two more pit stops for the girls and Renae said well Ken now you have had it. Why Ken asked? Renae said the sign back there read leaving New York and I believe it's illegal to transport young girls across a state line. He said you girls aren't young girls I know but with you I feel young again, me too Zenae said. Both girls were quiet for some reason as he drove on til it was evening and the sun had went down. The car came to a stop and the girls had been asleep off and on in another world. Renae said Ken where are we and why were you stopped pushing all those buttons? Zenae said my Sis, look it's our dream house when we were little girls. Renae said Sis you may of dreamed of a mansion, but I didn't. Zenae said Ken why are we here? Renae said Sis I don't care about the why we are here I want to meet the owners of all this. My look at all the pretty flowers and all the lovely trees that are blooming. Ken came to a stop where a man was doing something around the trees. Ken said the place looks real nice. The man said yes all of the flowers and trees are in full bloom. The man said I'll be up later. She's waiting for you and you know how she can get. Yes Ken said I know Dawn real well. The man said well just make her feel good. She's got it all ready for you and she loves it when you eat all you can of it. Ken said yes I hope it taste as good as it did the last time I ate it. The man said you know Dawn, she wants to make it better every time you eat. Ken said I better hurry I can't hardly wait to eat all I can of it, I'll see you later. The girls couldn't believe all they had heard, so Ken has got him a pussy away up here that he loves to eat, but when does he eat her pussy? Girls are you awake, I said let's go in and meet Dawn. Renae said what about our luggage, shouldn't we take our luggage in? Ken said leave them. Zenae said I was hoping this may be a bed and breakfast deal and I would get to stay in a real mansion just for once. Ken said it's not what you may think, let's meet Dawn. Ken and the girls walked up the walk and he pushed the buzzer for the door bell. A few minutes passed and the door opened. The girls just watched as a lovely black haired woman ran to Ken then she was up on him with both of her legs around his waist as she hugged and kissed him. Ken was even kissing her like he was ready to eat her. She climbed off of and said I'm so happy you are here, I've been waiting for you. She said Ken you know where your room is so go and show the girls the way, my Ken you have got two lovely girls here. Ken said Zenae and Renae this is Dawn and vice versa Dawn. Dawn said Ken I'll go get it ready for you to eat and I hope the girls will eat it too. Ken said I'm sure they will love it if they get a taste of it. She said oh my I can't wait for the girls to eat some of it, I'm gone. Ken led the girls through the house and down a hallway with paintings on both walls. The girls couldn't believe they were in a real mansion. Ken opened a door and said my girls this is our room. He stepped aside to let the girls enter. Zenae said Sis I couldn't begin to dream of all this. The girls walked around the large bedroom and Renae said Sis look here at what a bathroom. She said the bathroom is larger than our whole place back home. Renae said Sis you know what I'm thinking. Zenae said yes Sis you can't wait to get your pussy screwed in this big bed. Renae said heck I want to get Ken's dick all over this big room. Me too Sis but we have to talk in private about all we have heard. Yes Sis we sure do Renae said and Ken we are going to go look around and talk, don't get lost Ken said. Ken went out of the room when the girls left, he had some matters to check on. The girls found a room where they could have their long talk. They had their talk and they went back to the room. Ken said my girls come and get your shower, we have to go eat soon and Dawn's waiting for us. Renae said we don 't have any clean clothes to wear. Ken said look in the closet your luggage is there. Yes the girls figured Ken had carried all of their luggage in while they had their talk. The girls took their shower with Ken in a hurry and were out and dressed, sure no screwing. Ken got out and dressed and said my girls look lovely as always and started to kiss Zenae but she turned away and he got the same from Renae. He said it's time to go eat and Dawn has it hot and ready for us all to eat, let's go. Ken walked out of the room as the girls lagged behind on the walk. Ken stopped and said girls I know both of you really well and there's something wrong that I don't know. Girls Dawn has got it ready for us to eat and she's in there now waiting for us to eat it. Girls eat at least a little of it and try to please Dawn, now do as you may and at least put on a smile, let's go. Ken led the girls into a large room with the largest table they had ever seen and there was this Dawn woman and the man from the flowers, but he was a real nice looking man now. He said Ken you sit here and each lovely girl on each side of you.

Dawn said Ken it's hot the way you eat it and I hope the girls will like it too. The girls sat stunned at all the food that was on the table, of so many kinds of food. The girls had ate at a buffet restaurant years ago with their Mom and Dad but this wasn't a restaurant. Ken said Parker please say the blessing for our food. Both girls sat while the blessing was said and couldn't believe they were eating in this big mansion. Dawn brought the girls back when she said Ken serve the girls what they wish to eat. The girls didn't wish for to much to be put on their plates, they were sort of sick. The meal was ate and Ken took the girls back to their bedroom and he went into the bathroom for a while. The girls were sitting side by side on the bed when Ken came out of the bathroom. He kissed both girls and said I have some matters to take care of with Dawn, yes Parker also. He said don't wait for up me, you both look like you both need to get some rest after the drive up here, so good night and he walked out of the room. Renae said Sis there goes our screwing here in this big mansion. Zenae said yes Sis as hot as Dawn looks she will screw Ken's ass off all night. Renae said I wonder how he would feel if we were to screw this Parker fellow. Zenae said Sis I will never know how Ken will feel because all of my pussy will be all for Ken. Renae said Sis right now I'm not so sure about my pussy. Yes Sis my pussy did get sort of hot for this Parker fellow. Zenae said Sis your pussy got hot when we were young hot girls at home when the old dog catchers passed by our house. Yes Renae said back then I would have screwed him or the milkman. Zenae said Sis we never had a milkman, did we Sis. No Zenae said but I did when I lay and thought of getting my hot pussy screwed even by Mom's delivery man, let's go to bed. Ken shook the girls awake the next morning as they looked around the room. My girls let's take our shower and get ready to go eat breakfast. Dawn will have it all ready to eat and she loves to have it all ate, let's go. Renae said we will be there soon. Soon for the girls was after his shower. The girls took their shower and came out of the bathroom fully dressed. Zenae said I guess we are ready. Ken said I do hope you have your bags packed with all of your clothes and didn't leave any clothes in the bathroom as you both do at home. The girls saw that Ken's luggage was at the door. Zenae said I thought we would be here for awhile, we aren't packed. Ken said we move on, we have other places to see. Ken said this was just a one night thing for you girls the way you both have acted here. Ken finally got both girls and their luggage out of the room and the girls to there breakfast. Ken said Dawn you sure looked lovely last night as you do all the time. Dawn said girls just help yourselves and eat all you want. She said Ken you sure made me feel good after you ate so much last night. The girls looked at each other and now they were sure of it. Ken said Dawn that was good but not as good as you had ready for me to eat last night. Dawn said aw Ken you always say that it taste better every time you eat it. Ken said girls let's go wash and I'll tell Dawn bye at the door, you get your luggage and I'll be at the door. The girls washed and got their luggage and walked towards the door they had entered the night before. They saw it as plain as day what Ken and Dawn were doing. Dawn seems to like what Ken was doing for her. Ken said let's go my girls we have to travel. Dawn said not before I get my kiss. Renae said is that all you want from Ken? No Dawn said I would love for Ken to be here for me as he used to be, Ken's my man, now bye girls and be good to Ken. I'll tell Parker that you all said bye. They got their luggage loaded and the girls climbed in the back seat and buckled up. Ken began to drive and talk about their trip, but the girls weren't talking. He stopped for a fuel stop and a pee stop but the girls sat in their seats and pretended to be asleep. Ken drove on and late evening he stopped and the girls never moved out of their seats. Ken said girls the motel won't let you sleep in the car and if you want to know our room number is twelve. Oh yes it's right in front of us. Ken went in the room with his luggage and got a shower then got ready to go out and eat. The girls had never came in the room. He looked out to see if the girls were still in the car. He had forgot about the car's tinted windows and couldn't see in the car. Ken was going to a restaurant to eat, and the girls could do as they pleased. He drove around til he found the place he knew that would have the best to eat. The girls were glued to the back seat so he ate alone and then drove back to his room and went in and he soon was in his bed. Late in the night he woke up to a loud knock on his door. He went to the door and a big security guard stood there. He said Mr. Marshall do you know these girls, they say they are your girls. Ken said I know them as little brat Sisters. The security guard said Sir I don't care what they are but they can't sleep out in the car, now goodnight Sir. Thanks Ken said and brats go back and get your luggage or heck do as you please, I'm going back to bed. Ken woke up the next morning with both girls in bed with him. Now for the first time since they had slept with him, both girls were on the same side of the bed fully clothed. Ken just left time enough to check out then put the girls out of the bed, let's go girls we have to travel. But what about our shower they said. Ken said you must have took yours and got dressed before I did so let's ride. They wouldn't eat breakfast with Ken but he had his plans and he drove on with both bratty girls in the back seat. He knew this would most likely be the first and last trip with these brats. Ken said well girls you can get out or stay as you have been, I'm going to meet a lovely lady. The girls looked around and they couldn't believe it. They both sat stunned to be where they were. The back door was pulled open all of a sudden. Girls get your little bratty asses out, yes Ken has told me how you both have been on this trip. The girls sat and cried and said Mom we didn't plan to come back like this. No you little brats I don't believe planned to ever come back. Girls do as you always have done, just be little asses. Now Ken and I have a lot to talk about, we will be in the house girls. Zenae said Sis we had better go in as we are here. Renae said I don't know about all of this and she called him Ken. Zenae said let's go find out what we can about all of this. The girls went in the house they had grew up in and had been mostly brats while they grew up. Mom was so happy to see her girls but the girls weren't so happy and had very little to talk about. Out of the blue Renae said Ken we want to drive your car to go see an old friend. Ken said sure but I thought you would want to be with your Mom. We will be back in a couple of hours, Mom that will give you enough time for Ken to, well to get to know each other. Wait girls she said who are you going to see? One girl said it's Shanya and the other one said Susan, oh it's both Mom and we are gone. Ken I don't know about our girls, they can't lie any better for sure. Ken I guess you know what those brats have got on their mind for us don't you, yes I think I know. Ken said so do you want to do it now? Lenae said Ken I know my girls, well a Mother can tell what their girls are thinking. Ken those girls are parked some where plotting up another conniving plan to get you to screw my pussy. Ken another place and time I would try to screw your balls off. Ken I'm serious about my marriage vows. Ken you know how many years since my pussy has needed a dick. he just can't get it up any more and I still love him and I won't cheat. I thought it was me not being attractive anymore. I got dressed once to look like a pure slut, I wore the shortest in every thing I had and drove to another town. I went to see if I could attract a man but I didn't expect what I got and some wanted dates, others just wanted my pussy. Ken the security guard told me to leave the Mall before he called the Vice Squad to come get me. I left in shame of what I had done, I even so much as embarrassed myself on the drive home. Ken I looked down and saw a pair of hot pink panty's. I knew then I couldn't ever be a cheat. Ken the girls think they are real smart but one of the girls they went to see is dead. Shanya was killed in a car wreck out west where she and her family lived, she left a husband and two children. This Susie, she left before I ran the girls up off their asses and out of here. Susie went to work over in

China and married a wealthy Chinese man. Ken I can't screw you but let's put on a real good act for our girls. Ken said do you think it will help? No she said but it may help my pussy. She said Ken I bet those girls scream after you screw them, don't they? Yes they used to scream when we screwed. Ken before the girls come back I want to know if I can really can get you hard, will you let me try please and it's our act for the girls. Lenae took Ken's hand and led him to a bedroom and said it's the brats old room. Ken I need to go wash my pussy to do this, it's got wet. She said don't get undressed yet, wait for me please. Ken thought so this is where the girls layed and plotted and dreamed and got a hot pussy. I'm back Ken how do you like all you see? Ken I'm not as good looking as my girls but I bet I've got the freshest unused pussy, do you want to find out? Ken looked at a most lovely woman as she stood by the bed. My you are so lovely Lenae he said.

Ken before I go on as I've said before, I've only had one dick in my pussy, my husband's. Also it's my belief as it is with my husband that I can only cheat if I take your dick up in my pussy. Ken said why did you say my dick up in your pussy? Ken I guess it's that this is the closest to a hard dick in, well I told you the last time I screwed. Ken as I see it I can't screw but you do all the other you want to do. You know like sucking my titty's and kissing, oh yes play with my ass, I bet that I would love for you to do that for my ass. Heck Ken let me see my dick I've waited all this time to see. My your pants have filled out in front, I want to feel of my large dick you have for me. Ken said I thought you said no screwing? I can pretend yet Ken so let me do it, heck I'm going to get my pussy wet again. She began to pull Ken's clothes off from the top and she was shaking. Ken I never knew a dick could be so large, would he hurt my tight pussy, you know when he went in it, if he did? Ken pushed her naked lovely body back on the bed and looked at all the beauty she had. Ken began at the top and went down as she moaned. Now this she never knew about but she loved it. Ken had his mouth on her tasty pussy as he played with her ass as she moaned. Her clit was large and full and he began to tongue it as she moaned. Ken played with her ass and titty's, and she couldn't hold it. She gave a loud scream as he sucked her large clit. Her orgasms had never been such as this man had just gave her, he made her come over and over as she screamed. Ken let her rest and she lay with a dreamy look in her eyes. Ken that was my best that I've ever had, you want to do some more? Ken can a man put his dick up to my pussy, just to the edge and not go all the way in? Ken said you want to feel me shoot off in your pussy don't you? Ken it would make me the happiest ever, do you shoot off a lot, it don't matter just shoot my pussy full but don't go in my pussy. Ken I can't cheat no matter how good you make my pussy feel. Ken you better skip the mouth on my pussy deal, it's real wet. Ken just do all you want and make me scream all you want. Ken let me hold your dick before I get him wet with my pussy, now don't go all the way in, please. Ken said you know how much dick it takes for you to cheat so you take all you want. Thanks Ken and I love you and your dick, now screw or let me get what I want and not cheat. He let her have all she wanted and he felt her pussy begin to work on his dick head and this couldn't last. He got a finger on her clit as she worked her pussy. She gave a loud scream as she got what she wanted for her pussy. She pulled his lips to her and gave him a long kiss. Ken that was the best that I've ever had, we weren't cheating either. She got out of bed and said I've got to wash my pussy I want some more like that one.

She came back and said I see he's hard and he's so big and how lovely, now make my pussy feel you shoot it full again. Oh my love I need all I can get up in my pussy and I'll help all I can. She was hungry for his dick and easy to come and he shot her pussy full as she screamed. Ken I've got to wash my pussy again, the next one we will have to pretend for the girls. He said do you want me to wash your pussy? Ken you will be the first man to even see it and I would love to let you wash my pussy. Ken gave her two hot ones in the bathroom as he washed her hot pussy. Ken here I go and I have never done this for any man. That didn't take her long til she got what she wanted. Ken I love you for all you have done for me and my girls. Now let's get ready for them, I heard them drive up. The girls walked in the door as they heard their Mother scream. The girls looked at each other and Renae said Ken has tore our Mom's pussy apart with his big dick.

Zenae said yes I remember how small Dad's dick is and we were little girls then, there she's screaming again. The girls sat down in the livingroom to wait. Zenae said reckon Ken's dick has killed our Mom, oh here she comes out now. Lenae came out wearing only her bathrobe and said oh you girls are back early. Where's Ken Mom Zenae asked? Oh he's back there somewhere, he's not a mouse catcher I've found out. Renae said why are you in your bath robe Mom? Girls I didn't want to come out here naked. I never come out of the shower and walk around naked. Renae said Mom what's Ken taking so long back there for? Renae why not go back and ask Ken, oh here he comes. Lenae said Ken I hope you got rid of that mouse, I'm going to have to set out more traps I guess. Renae said Ken what's with you coming out with your shirt out of your pants, your face is awfully red too? Ken said girls just why were you gone for so long, now

I bet you went out to look up your old boyfriends. My I hope you girls didn't do anything in my car with your friends, I'm going out and check out my car now. Renae said Mom Ken's face was awfully red so is yours. Now what went on here whlle me and my Sis were gone? Lenae said why not go ask the mouse that Ken was after, maybe then you may know. Ken said girls I'm going to get a room and take a shower after that fight with that wild animal that scared your Mom, then I'm going to go eat. Renae said wait are you coming back here later? Why Ken asked I brought you girls here to see your Mom and Dad and where have you two been as we sat here and waited. Zenae said now I hope we can come back when Dad comes home to see him. Lenae said Ken if you will and they want to, bring them back after you eat, now kiss me bye, not you girls, you Ken. Renae said now that's real dandy Ken, we leave you alone with our Mom for ten minutes and you rape her. Ken,

Mom's pussy I know you sure tore it apart with your big dick, Mom's never screwed a big dick before. Yes Zenae said Dad never made our Mom scream as loud as you did. Ken said girls run your bratty mouths while I check us in for a room. Renae said you could have took Mom to a motel room and screwed her. Sis I bet he screwed her in our room. Zenae said it doesn't matter to me now after he's went and screwed Mom's ass off. Ken said girls didn't you two get your pussy's screwed after you left me with your Mom? No we didn't Ken. Both girls ran their mouth on Ken about how he had tore their Mom's pussy up with his big dick. Ken said girls get dressed and ready to go eat and then go meet your Dad. Girls if you are going with me I'll give you twenty minutes to get ready to go with me. Zenae said make that a half hour. Ken said no let's make that fifteen minutes and I'll go meet your Dad without you two little brats. Ken said your time has started and you haven't, wait for us Ken Renae said, you want to go wash our pussy's for us? No I don't at this time but I will wait and put clean panty's on for both of you. Yes and you can just forget that and our pussy's too Renae said. He said if you can be ready in fourteen minutes lock the door when you come out, if not don't come out I'll be gone. It was warm weather but Ken got it cold from the girls til they arrived at their parent's home. Renae said Ken if you can just try to keep your hands off our Mom, at least don't let Dad see you if you do. Lenae met them at the door and said Ken the little brats did come back to see their Dad, come in the livingroom. Girls I'll go get your Dad, he brought his work home with him as usual. The girls didn't expect to see their Dad as they saw him as they went to him and gave him a hug. Lenae said Sydney this is Kenneth Marshall, our girls full time nanny. Ken and Sydney shook hands and talked for a while and Lenae said Ken let's go in the kitchen and let the girls and their Dad catch up on what they have been up to for the last few years. Lenae said Ken Sydney and me are the same age but we sure don't look like it now. He was my first and only boyfriend. As I told you before his dick was the only dick ever for me. Ken he looks so old and I can't get him to slow down in his work. I don't know what to do to help him. Ken had seen plenty of men like Sydney that seemed to be afraid to slow down that if they did they wouldn't get started again. They would work themselves into an early grave. She said Ken thanks for what all you did for me today and I need more. Ken let's go outside and I'll show you my little garden, oh come on it won't take long. It didn't take long after they went outside til she held his dick as he gave her what she needed. I hope I never screamed, I bit into my hand, oh Ken my pussy needed that, now kiss me.

Please Ken suck my titty's once more and do me with your fingers, oh yes, my how good you make me and my pussy feel. Oh yes what about my girls, have you screwed them since you all left here. Ken said no they both have went to having their periods at the same time and I'm not sure how long they will last, maybe as much as two months or til they get ready for me. She said they sure are brats, let's go back and wake Sydney up, it's past his bedtime. Sydney had went to bed Renae said. Zenae said Mom where have you and Ken been, we couldn't find you two. Lenae said I took Ken outside to show him my vegetable garden. Zenae said Mom we are going to leave and tuck Ken into bed, it's past his bedtime. They all got hugs and kisses and Mom got more when the girls left her alone with Ken. The brats were still riding in the back seat and they weren't talking. Ken said girls you can get out of the car and get in our room or stay out here, yes if another security man wakes me up with you two brats I don't know you, good night girls. They followed Ken in his room and the girls began to run their mouth. Zenae said where were you and Mom while we talked to Dad? Renae said Sis you know where they were, Ken took Mom out behind the house and raped Mom's pussy again. Yes he took her outside where we couldn't hear Mom scream as he had her screaming today. Zenae said I bet Mom's little pussy is not so little now. Renae said Sis I don't think Dad will ever know how bad Ken has tore up Mom's little pussy. Ken said good night girls. Ken drove back home with the two brats only making two motel stops. It was a cold icy ride back home from both girls. The girls slept with Ken but they must have lost their pussy's somewhere before they had started the trip. Ken stopped at their place and told the girls to take their luggage and get out. Renae said we will take your luggage up to our room.

Leave it, Ken said I'll take care of it, yes and don't wait up for me, I've got some important matters to take care of. Zenae said now what sort of matters would Ken have to take care of? Renae said Sis I don't care what Ken does so let's go take our showers and go to bed. It was Wednesday evening and Ken had some matters that he had to work on his own. He was never a person to just sit at home and do nothing so he got busy at his paper work to keep it caught up. Ken went home Sunday morning after he ate breakfast to a messy place. He saw that the girls must have forgot to clean up the kitchen after they ate. He went to put away his clothes and found the girls dirty clothes just scattered on the floor. He left their clothes as they were and put his away. Both girls were under the bed covers asleep. Ken went to the bathroom to take a pee and wash his hands. The girls clothes were scattered all over the bathroom floor, some were wet and had been walked on and they smelled. Ken went to the bed and tried to wake the girls. Renae woke up first and said oh it's you, what do you want, if it's our pussy's you can forget it, and now leave us alone. Ken said girls this place is a complete mess, it looks like two little brats have left a mess. Girls I'm packing my bag and leave you two brats in your mess, bye. Ken went to his office on Monday morning and got to work to catch up his office paper work. He called each department head to find out if all went smooth while he was gone. Zenae's vacation replacement answered the phone and Ken said how's your department doing today? Oh it's going okay for me. He said Zenae must be taking another week off. Ken said why's that? He said she nor Renae came back to work today. Ken said well just keep it all running smoothly. Ken went home to find both girls in bed asleep. The place was still in a mess. He took a shower and shook the girls awake. Zenae said now what do you want from us? Ken said first I want my place cleaned up then I will discuss what I want next. Renae said Ken you can't tell us what to do so buzz off. Ken said girls I will make this plain for you two brats. Ken said our place is a mess that you two brats have made then layed on your asses, next you two didn't show up for work today. The mess you made you can clean up, that is when you get out of your little girl panty's. Yes your position with my company I'm not sure about. If you girls knew your position as I do you would know that as of now the process to fire both you is moving up to my office. Why you may wonder, I'll tell both of you. It's company policy to discharge any employees that fail to be at work or doesn't call. Now you know where that leaves the two of you. Ken said girls that's all I have to say. Ken packed his luggage and said I'll clean out the rest of all I have here tomorrow. Ken started to walk out with his luggage. Wait Zenae said where are you going? Ken said to a clean room, this room stinks and both of you stink. Ken walked out and checked into another room. Zenae said see Renae what you have done. Renae said you helped make all of this mess. Zenae said I'm going to clean up my part of this mess and I don't know about our jobs. Renae said aw Ken he was just blowing as usual. Zenae said I'm going to clean up my part and go to work in the morning. It wasn't easy to get back to work the next day. The Personnel Director had both girls in his office one at a time. It was late in the afternoon when Zenae had climbed up to Ken's office the wrong way. Ken said Miss it's been sent to me that you failed to be at work as you were to be. No call to be excused did you make. Miss I have many duties with my title, one is to decide to discharge you or not, now what do you have to say? Zenae said oh Ken let's not make a big deal out of this. Miss, to you I'm Mr. Marshall and it's a big deal. Now what do you have to say? Zenae said oh nothing, but I think you are being a big ass. Anything else Ken asked? No Ken Zenae said and you are being an ass about this. Ken said you may wait out in the waiting room and do as you may as I make my decision. Renae was let in another door to Ken's office after Zenae had went out. Ken said it's been made aware to me that you failed to be in your department on your work day. You made no call to be excused and a person in your position should know is a course for your termination. He said the hardest thing for me to do is to fire anyone but I have to make that decision as bad as I hate to do it. Now Miss do you wish to say anything to explain your past actions? Renae said aw Ken cut out the big boss act so I can go home. Miss he said to you I'm Mr. Marshall and if you have nothing to say you may leave. Yes Miss the Personnel Director will let you know of my decision. Renae said what about our jobs, I mean my job. Ken said Miss if you have any personal belongings here get them on your way out. Yes you are as of now suspended with out pay for two weeks. Yes you may leave now, yes on the way out don't slam my door. Yes tell your Sister to come back in my office. Renae said you tell her yourself Ken. Ken said all of this will be on your permanent work file. Renae walked out and Zenae said what did he say to you Sis? Renae said oh it was all a bunch of bull, oh yes Sis I got us two weeks of vacation we didn't know about. Zenae said wow Sis that's really great. Renae said oh yes that's two weeks without pay. Zenae said now what did Ken say about our jobs? Sis as of now we don't have a job and Ken will decide what to do about the matter. Zenae said Ken didn't tell me all of that. Renae said maybe Ken just forgot to tell you, let's go home. The girls had plenty of time to clean up their messy place, and lay around and be bored. The Personnel man talked to each girl on Friday evening on their second week at home. They were to meet Mr. Marshall in his office at eight am the next Monday morning. Renae said that's to early to be at the office. He said then I take it you don't wish to even know what Mr. Marshall's decision will be about your job. Renae said aw I guess I'll be there. He said Ma'am I take it you don't think very much of your work here. Oh I guess I'll go see Ken Monday morning, bye he said. Zenae said Sis what time do you have to be in Ken's office? Renae said the Personnel man said to be there at eight am but that's to early for me. Zenae said that's the time he told me to be there. Renae said I believe that the company is just pushing us to hard, I guess I'll sleep late on Monday morning. Zenae said Sis I believe we have pushed to much this time. Renae said you do know we have plotted and planned together since we were little so we will always stay together. Zenae said Sis I think this time we have pushed to hard. Renae said oh Ken will just give us a little talk and act like the big CEO of the company. Zenae said Sis Ken is the CEO of the company. Renae said Sis by now Ken will be ready to screw our pussy's and he will be ready to screw us right in his office, I bet he will. Both girls went in Kenneth's office on time together. Ken said girls sit down and let me talk straight to you. To begin with this isn't personal, this is all business. Ladies I've gone over your recent performance records and it's not good. I don 't know what you ladies have been up to but it's not helped you or your departments. You are not putting the effort into the positions you were in charge of. I have went over your performance records as I said and you both have dropped the ball. I have made my decision about what I have to do for you both and for the company.

I give you the choice, you may go back to your departments but you both will be demoted back to where you were before you were promoted last. That's it and you may walk out and I'll give you fifteen minutes to make your decision. Oh yes ladies all of this will be on your permanent records. Oh yes rent is due this Friday. Now go and do some more of your conniving plots and make a choice of what you want to do with your lives. Renae said Sis he can't push us around as he thinks, I won't put up with this. Zenae said we have ten minutes to decide. Renae said I don't know what to do after the way Ken did us on our vacation. Zenae said Sis maybe we should have talked to Ken about the way he did us. Renae said then you want to give Ken another chance? Zenae said no I believe we should thank Ken for giving us another chance. She said this time we will have to give in and like it. Renae said I don't like it but let's wait til the last minute before we give in to Ken, maybe he will want our pussy by then. Ken said you seem not to like the decision you made. He said let me tell you both that you both can be replaced in a heart beat by people with a better attitude than you have and more qualified. Girls if you are serious about your decision meet me at this address at four pm this evening. Why should we do that for you Renae said? For one I gave you a choice and two, you will be on company time. Now believe it or not I have work to do and you two may leave now. Both girls left mad at Ken for the way he had done them. Zenae said Sis we had better meet him as he asked this evening. Oh Renae said Ken just wants to get us out of this building and brow beat us and I won't put up with his bull. Zenae said we better meet him on his time. Yes I guess we better, do you have the address to meet him, no you have it, no you have it. The girls met Ken at a cafe in a part of the city they had never been. Ken said girls let's

order and eat, I'm paying. The girls
never ate much but Ken ate a good
meal, he made the meal last a way to
long the girls thought. Ken said girls
if you need to pee go do it while I pay
for our meals, I'll wait for you. All three
took a ride in a taxi to a place out to the
edge of the city. Ken said let's go for
a walk girls. The sun had left the city
as the girls lagged behind Ken. A young
man came out of a small building and
said Ken I'm still hoping. Ken said Philip
don't give up hope, I've not. Ken walked
on and a young woman came out of a
small building and said thanks
Mr. Marshall, I got it. Ken said June I told
you it would work out and here you know
what you need to do. Ken placed some
bills in the woman's hands. She hugged
Ken's neck and said I have to do this
and she kissed Ken's lips, thanks again
and she wiped her eyes. Ken said just
do your best now bye. They walked on
as Ken talked to many women and men.
Ken said girls I better let you go home

so you can change each other's diapers. They arrived back at the girl's place and he said I've lost some items, I may have left them up in you girl's place. I'll go up and look if it's alright with you two girls. Zenae said it's our place and you know that, let's go Ken. He didn't find the items at the place. Ken said this place we just came from is a homeless shelter, a place that you two would know little about. Ken said girl's let's go in your living room and set down for a while and talk. Renae said I'm not sure I want to talk, then listen Ken said. Ken said girl's what did you see at the shelter? Renae said I saw a lot of bummy people looking for a handout. Yes Zenae said I never saw any that I would ever want to meet again. Ken said that's what I thought you both would see. Girls listen if you want to, please. Some years back a young man had dreams of being a big success in business. He worked and saved as did his parents, his Dad worked two jobs, his Mother did laundry for anyone she could. He went to a six year term in college to get his degrees. His Dad passed away in the young man's fifth year at school. He was ready to drop out and go home to take care of his dear Mom. His Mom pushed him to get all the degrees that he would need to land a good job. He as a lot of people had sent out resumes to any company that he could. No big job at the end of his college, he went home to his Mom and layed down and waited for a reply to his resume's. His Mom died leaving him the small home they lived in. He didn't know it but the home had been mortgaged to put him through college. He left the only home he ever knew and went on the road. he had no address to receive his mail if there were any. He came to this city and went to every place he could get in. Time goes on but he was stuck in the mud. The shelters were all full and he slept when and where he could. This young man was near ready to jump off of a building to get out of his mess. He had a drive to make a success but he had lost his will to go on. One day these ladies from a church came to where he and others like him lived in card board boxes. These nice women brought meals for the bums as they were to eat, this young man was no bum but he was hungry. A young lady gave him his meal and their hands touched. For the first time in his life there was some thing inside of him that moved and there was a fire he had never known in him. The meals came from the women and the young girl and this homeless man felt something but what could they do. He couldn't do very much but she did. She gave him a drive he needed. She helped him to get out of the gutter and get him in a room with clothes for a job interview. She was an angel on earth. He went to work and he did work with a passion. Yes the young man and woman married and lived in a small one bedroom apartment and walked to and from work. He had never met her family and she never talked of them. She had a passion for going out to help people. He went home one evening from work and she was crying. He hugged her and said what's wrong? Her Father had passed away and she hadn't took time to go see her Dad or Mom for years. They rode a bus up state to catch a ride to her home. There was a car at the bus station waiting for them. She ran to the car's driver and hugged him and said Henry how's Mom? He said let's ride and talk on the way home. He was the family chauffeur and butler and all around man. He drove forever it seemed and stopped at a large house and said I'll bring your bags in, go to your Mom. Her Mom was as loving as she was and she was a most lovely woman. The funeral passed and the couple had to go back to work. It wasn't long til her Mother passed on, one weekend as his wife was out helping out a homeless shelter. Another trip for a funeral and all that was left at the big house were the butler and cook that was the maid's housekeeper and all that she could be. His wife spent all of her free time at the church's or shelters helping those in need. His dear wife got sick at work and was sent to the emergency room. After tests were run over and over he got the news. His wife had incurable brain cancer and he was at a loss at what he could do for her. There was nothing he could do but be with her all that he could. Time passed and she got worse in health each day. She had inherited all that her parents owned and she made her will out to leave all she had to him. She just went away farther each day. This loving kind woman said on her last day, promise you will be of help to those who are in need as long as you can. His dear wife went away the next day as he held her hand. He had lost all he had to live for but it wasn't what he had promised his love he would do. He picked up where she left off. One night at the shelter he met a lady that was at her end. She never had a load of degrees but she was a smart woman and he saw that she left with a job. He helped all that he could, he never seemed to help all that he wanted to. One young man that had been a landscaper had lost all he had in the recession, he got him out of the shelter with a job. this young man's name was Parker and then there was Dawn, they were working at the same place and yes they fell in love and now are very much married and happy. Oh yes she found out she was pregnant a few weeks ago. My girls I have done all I can do to help you and I'll never give up on you but you both are still little selfish ass brats. Girls if you leave this world as you have been you will leave with a frown. Girls there's more to life than you two will ever learn about with the attitude that you both have. You didn't get it from your Mom, she's a most loving kind woman, now I'm going home, well it's my home in the city. Renae said Ken you tell us what all of what you just said have to do with you eating this girl Dawn's pussy, then stay up late in the night screwing her on our trip? Ken said how do you know that I did any of what you said? Zenae said Ken after you saw this fellow Parker all we heard was you eating Dawn's pussy. Ken said girl's I never heard one thing about Dawn's pussy up there and sure no screwing it. Zenae said where were you for all that time? Girls do you remember all the food that was on the table before we ate up there? Girls Dawn loves to cook, she cooks my favorite foods when I go up there. Yes girls I ate what Dawn had cooked for me. Now all the food that Dawn and Parker had on the table didn't go to waste, and as I said after we came back to your room. You two girls wasted enough food to feed a homeless man for two weeks. Ken said when I left you two that night I went to the dining room where Parker and Dawn were busy. We took all the left over food that Parker and Dawn had prepared to a homeless shelter. It was a little late to eat but when a person is hungry it don't matter when, time doesn't matter. Zenae said and you never ate Dawn's pussy or screwed her pussy. Ken said girls Dawn's a good girl and no I've only been a help to her. What about our Mom when we left you two alone and came back and heard her screaming and both of you out of your clothes. Ken said girls you need to ask your Mom about all of that. Renae said Ken we know you screwed our Mom but we wanted you to screw our Mom. Ken said girls you know the girls you went to visit up there were dead, no you go at all you do with a blind eye and you just don't care. Zenae said then you tell us why you stopped screwing our pussy's? Girl's it's like this, you both began to

have your periods at the same time
that hasn't stopped, well as far as I
know it's not. Both of you went to bed
fully dressed on the same side of the
bed. Yes so close to the side of the bed
that you took turns rolling out of the bed
each night. On our road trip you acted
like spoiled brats, you both sat in the
back seat and hardly ever spoke. One
hotel guard was ready to have you both
locked up for vagrancy. When we got
back here I wanted to give you two the
chance to get the bug out of your asses.
I went that night and did all of my
laundry and went to my new home. You
two know about your jobs and how assy
you were. I came here and never had
seen or smelled the such, you both were
stinking as bad as your place was.
He said it was a mess from the kitchen
to all over the place. Clothes laying
where you left them in the floor. I went
in the bathroom and it wasn't any better,
I picked up your panty's off the floor
where you had been walking on them.

I always loved the pussy aroma of your panty's but these stunk. Where were you, both of you were in the bed asleep and you both stunk, and you know what time of day it was. Girls I had never smelled any homeless person to stink as bad as you were. Renae said how did you know where my parent's lived. Girls that has nothing to do with this, I'll tell you I'm not all dumb and I checked your employee record. Yes your Mom and me had talked by phone a few times before we made our trip. Ken said girl's that's the way it is as of now. Renae said Ken are you going to screw our pussy's tonight? No and bye girls. For some time all Ken knew about the girls were their performance records and at least they have started moving up again. One day he took a phone call from Lenae. She said Ken he's gone, he died at the office. He said I'm sorry. She said he wouldn't listen to me and he pushed himself to hard. Ken I really need you at this time. I have no one up here except a few of his friends. Ken said I'll be up there tomorrow evening. He said have you told the girls yet? No Ken I've not talked to the girls since I saw them up here last. He said neither girl has called you? No and I tried the number you gave me but it was a dead number. Ken I don't know why the girls won't talk to me but will you tell the girls about their Dad, and I love you. Ken just tell them you are going to be up here, it's up to them of what they do, bye Ken. Ken met both girls as they were leaving the building after work. Zenae said Renae he is still alive. Yes she said and now what are you wanting from us this time, not one of your tours to the bum places is it? Ken said girls I want to talk to you at your place. Renae said I guess you are hard up for a pussy and now you want ours. Well Ken we don't have any pussy to give you. Ken said here's my taxi, get your own and if it's not a big bother to you girls I'll meet you in the lobby at your place if you want to, I'm gone. Renae said Sis we will get us a different dick tonight, Kens'. Zenae said I'm mot sure I want to give Ken my pussy. Yes Renae said we just left our best dicks back there in our departments. Zenae said do you want to meet with Ken or not? I say not Renae said, me to Sis. Ken sat and waited for the girls for near an hour and no show. He had ways to reach all of the employees in upper management and he ate then went to his place and called the girls. Ken had planned to leave the city early the next morning to drive up to be with Lenae, he called the girls near midnight and no answer. The next morning early he gave the girls another call but got no answer. Ken made another try then he went to the girl's place and knocked on the door for near five minutes, off and on. The girls were asleep and couldn't be woke up or they weren't home. He would call their department later on, after his drive up to Lenae's. Ken was at Lenae's late in the evening. She said I'm so glad you came up to be with me. He said I'm sorry about the girls but as I told you last night I tried. Ken I don't know if those girls will ever grow up and get out of their diapers. They sat and talked til up in the night and she said Ken I would love for you to go to bed with me now but we can't now as you know. Yes Lenae I know but I will always be here for you as long as you want or need me, now I'll see you at the funeral home tomorrow. Ken will you please hold me in your arms before you leave? Ken held her in his arms and she said I better let you go as we are, bye my love. Ken met her at the funeral home the next day to be with her. The funeral plans were already made so there wasn't much to do. She said the girls should have called from work by now, shouldn't they Ken? Yes he said if they went to work today. She said can they just take off work when they please? No he said they can't. He said I'll do some calling to see how things are going at work. The next day Ken placed a call to Zenae's department office and was told that Zenae had called in that she was sick. He called Renae's department and she had called in as being sick the last three days. He hoped there weren't a virus going around. He met Lenae at the funeral home and got behind her car in a short funeral procession and a short ride. A Minister said his words and then what few friends were there were gone. She said Ken do you believe that both girls would be sick at the same time? He said yes it's possible. She said I don't believe that either one was or is sick. Ken those girls like to plot and be little asses that are conniving. She said you aren't dumb to all the girl's plots I know. Ken said all I can do is believe them til it's proved different. Lenae said let's go home, I meant my home and eat and talk. They went to her home and ate and sat and talked til late in the night. She said I've never got any of this before and I love you and I thank you for being here for me. The next morning he hugged her bye and she gave him a kiss on his cheek. She said you know all we talked about and did last night and call when you get home. You see if you can find what's wrong with them girls besides being asses. Ken drove home without any motel stops and called to check on the girls. He found out that both girls had called in sick for the past three days. He got a phone number the girls had gave for their record where they could be reached. Both girls of course had the same number. Ken called and got a, this number is no longer in service. Ken soon was at his old place knocking on the door. Well Zenae said Ken I thought you were dead. Renae said he doesn't look to well, maybe he is dead. Ken said do you girls always answer your door half naked? No Renae said sometimes we are all naked, they both laughed. Ken said girls

I need to talk to both of you but your place stinks bad and so do both of you. He said if I may come in, go get some clothes on before we talk. Renae said we will put our panty's on if we can find some that are clean. He said I'm going to use your restroom if you don't mind. The girl's place was in a mess again as it was before. Renae said okay Ken what do we talk about? Ken said first you both have called in sick at work for the past three days. Neither one of you act as if you are sick or have been for the past three days. Next why do you have a number at work listed as your contact number that is no longer in service? Renae said I didn't know about that, did you Sis? No Zenae said I didn't know and they both sat and giggled with their legs up under their asses as little young girls may do. He said girls your place is in a mess as before. They giggled for a while then laughed. Renae said Ken our damn place has not one thing to do with our work, so butt out.

Ken said girls what if you needed to be contacted in case of an emergency? Renae said me and Sis are always close together and always will be. Ken said girls I tried calling your number and got no answer, all I got was that your number was no longer in service. Renae said see Sis I told you Ken was dumb and he proved it by calling a number more than once that was no longer in service. Ken said girls I came here to talk to you last Monday and you never answered the door. He said I waited in the lobby til after midnight and you never did come home. I came by the next morning and still got no answer at your door. Renae said maybe you should have knocked louder, shouldn't he Sis? They laughed til their titty's flopped out of their gown. Renae said look at what you have caused, our puppies have got loose. They sat and giggled as their large titty's bounced up on their chest. Renae said Sis I caught my puppies. You can suck mine Ken but no pussy will you get. Ken said girls your Father is dead and buried. Zenae said why didn't Mom call us? Yes Renae said that's just like Mom. Ken said listen you smart asses, why didn't you call your Mom? Girls you haven't spoke to your Mom since I brought you back from your trip up there. You girls have shown no concern for your Mom and Dad that I have seen. But Zenae said what does any of this have to do with our work? Ken said girls I'm going home to do some work and get some rest. Oh yes as a person in your position at work you know that if any employee missed three days of work, the employee must provide a legal doctor's excuse for the days in question. Girls I hope you two haven't lost your doctor's excuses, my all the mess you have in your place, now goodnight. Zenae said now Sis what are we going to do about our doctor's excuses? Renae said Ken's bluffing us or trying to, we go to work Monday.

They went and were soon in the Personnel Directors office. Girls in the position you have with our company you know the rules, as you should know. If you wish to return to work you bring me a legal doctor's excuse for all three days you have called in sick and that is for all the time you miss work. I have work to do unlike some of our departments or so you two may think, now come back as I have said or you won't work here. Yes Renae said we will wait and see about that. Out on the street Zenae said now what Sis? Oh let's see what I can find out about the what the other's did, I mean do for a doctor's excuse. Well Sis now we have dug us a deep hole this time Zenae said. Renae had to make several phone calls to get all the information she needed to call a doctor's office. The girls hit a lucky streak and they got an early canceled out appointment that Friday at four pm. After begging and crying the doctor wrote the girl's excuses to cover their asses. Yes the girl's doctor would do a followup the next night in their room. The girls got by that deal and now they needed Ken to move back in with them. After several weeks had passed with the girls calling and begging for Ken to move back. Ken said meet me at this address for lunch or whatever you call it but it's for seven pm tonight. Renae said Sis we have to get Ken back in our place to make our plan work. Ken I'm sure will be crazy for our pussy as he used to be. Zenae said are you sure our plan will work? Yes Renae said. The girls were let out of the taxi at the restaurant that Ken said they would meet. They went into the place and were met by a nice hostess. She said ladies is this table for a party of two? No Ma'am we are to meet a friend here, a Mister Marshall. Oh yes Mr. Marshall is waiting for you, follow me. They followed the hostess through the long dining area to the back where Ken was waiting. The hostess said Mr. Marshall these ladies say they are friends of yours? Ken said the friend part I'm not sure about their part but I was to meet them here. She said Mr. Marshall your waitress will take your order. Ken said give us a half an hour to go over our menus and thanks Sherrie. Renae said well Ken you must eat here a lot since you ran out on me and Sis. Ken said what makes you say all that you just said? Oh Ken you just called the hostess by her name, Ken you did run out on me and Sis. Ken said I do eat here as often as I can and I do know most of the employees that work here, I do believe that I left you two girls when you tried to live like slobs, I won't live like that. Ken said now how do you two like your old place? Zenae said how do you mean our old place? Ken said you girls don't remember your Uncle Bob's barber shop. Yes Renae said but it was a real small shop. Ken said yes girls that's all that you two saw. Girls when I told you that I would help on the sale of the property that Bob had, I did. At the time there was no sale so the Realtor bought your property, and I later bought it from the Realtor. Now here's our waitress so let's order and we will talk as we eat. Zenae said now Ken why did you buy Uncle Bob's barber shop as you said you did? Ken said girls I saw something that Bob and I wanted to do. Girls Bob and I helped all we could at our homeless shelter as much as we could. Girls Bob and I had plans of how we could help more people. Bob owned more space here than the barber shop. Yes Bob owned all of this plus a full size kitchen in back. All the people that work here or has worked here came from the shelter or from off the streets. I had project engineers and planners to lay out all of Bob's place and I know Bob would be proud of it. Some come here til they can get a better place to work then they train their replacements then they move on to a better place where they can use their degrees they went to college for. I can just see Bob as each person goes to work and then again as the person moves on to another job. Renae said but why Ken do all of this? Ken said girls I don't guess you will ever know. Mr. Marshall may I get your party anything else, the baker has the best chocolate cake ever. No thanks Jasmine I'll pass this time. She said ladies do you want desert? No Zenae said we are full, thanks. Ken said Jasmine I hear that you are moving on. Yes Ken or I mean Mr. Marshall and I could hug you again for helping me to get the job. Ken said Jasmine I only gave you a break you needed, you got the job on your own. Ken said Jasmine I gave you what I have gave to others. Some I've helped seemed to have forgot or just don't care. Jasmine said oh Ken I'll never forget and I do love you for all you do to help all of those you can. Now I better get to work, bye. Renae said I bet you have screwed her pussy a lot since you ran out on me and Sis haven't you Ken? Ken said is that all you think I'm about? Renae said no Ken Sis and I know that you are a good man to help the people that you do. Heck Ken Renae said Sis and I want you to move back to your place, we miss you. Zenae said Ken I miss you but I do miss the only dick that ever gave me pleasure. Ken said girls you both are to lazy and messy for me to live with. Renae said Ken we can clean up your place as it used to be. Ken said girls call me when you get the place as clean as it was when I let you both move in. Renae said heck that will take us all weekend. Zenae said Sis I want to get Ken's dick back in my pussy before the weekend is over. Renae said yes my pussy wants Ken's large dick up in it now. Zenae said Sis let's go home and let's get the place clean. Yes Renae said, yes my pussy is hot for the first time since you ran out on us. Ken said girls call me when you think it's clean and I'll come over and inspect the place. Zenae said bring your bags and dick and be ready to screw us. Let's go Sis we have some cleaning to do. Ken had to say bye to Jasmine before he left. She looked at the bills Ken had put in her hand and she said Ken I can't give you the young pussy that your young friends have but I would give you all I have but I'm not that kind of girl. Ken said yes I know as I'm not that kind of man. Jasmine said Ken if you have helped those two girls as you have helped others you better watch out, Ken those girls are mean girls. Ken said Jasmine if you ever need me, call me, now bye. Ken went to his place and packed a bag for the weekend. Ken knew the girls would bust their asses to get his dick. Renae called the next morning early and said Ken we have got it clean, yes she said our pussy's are clean too, come on please. Ken just took enough clothes to get started to work on Monday. He sure hoped the place was clean, the girl's had good pussy's or did have. Zenae said Sis and I busted our asses to clean up the place to get you to move back in here. Ken said I'll look the place over before I set my bag down. Renae said I hope the place will pass your inspection. Ken went over the place and said girls you have got the place clean once again. Now will you screw our hot pussy's Renae asked? Ken said girls if I screw your pussy's for you, how long will this place stay clean? He said if I move back and you two mess this place up again I'm gone for good from here. Renae said Ken we promise we won't be lazy asses. Ken said I mean all I've said. Now have you talked to your Mom? Zenae said it's been quite a while, we have been busy. Ken said girls don't ever be to busy to talk to your Mom. Renae said oh we will call her soon won't we Sis. Yes Zenae said but for now Ken we want your dick up in our pussy's. In bed as they all lay naked as they all had done before,

Renae said Ken which one do you want to screw first? It's no matter to me he said. Zenae said I guess we get to decide who Ken screws first, you ready Sis? Wait Ken said none of all that you two did the first time we screwed. Zenae said I guess his dick is really full and I've got the smallest pussy so it won't hold all of his dick juice, you go first. Renae said I guess I better go first for his dick feels real full. Zenae said Sis that's my arm you are holding. Oh my I hope Ken's dick hasn't grown to big for our pussy's. Ken said girls I don't believe either one of you are wanting to screw my dick, so let's go to sleep. Ken said I guess you both have got you a better dick to screw since I left you two with your mess you had made. Renae said I believe you lived here and you made most of the mess that you left here, isn't that right Zenae? Yes Sis Zenae said, most of this mess was his. Ken said move Renae I'm getting out of the bed. She said I guess we got your dick hard and you have to pee don't you? He said the hard dick part you got right, now move. He got out of the bed and begun to get dressed. Zenae said Ken what are you doing? He said I'm getting dressed then going to my place, oh yes I'll take a pee first. But why Renae asked? Ken never answered, he went to take a pee before he left. Zenae said Sis we had better do something, we never thought it would go this way. Zenae said Sis we can't let Ken get away from us this time, you know how much we need him and his dick. He came back to get his bag to leave and said girls when will you learn there's more than just a pussy and dick. He said I do know your Mom is right about you two, you both are plotters and liars and conniving and little assed brats. I kept this place clean as we lived here as you two tried to live like pigs. How long had I been gone and come back to the messy place that you both made. Zenae said oh Ken don't leave us we need you to stay, isn't that right Sis? Yes Renae said I'm sorry for trying to blame you for the mess we made. Zenae said come back to bed Ken we really do need you for more than your dick, don't we Sis? Ken went back to bed that night but he didn't give the girls his dick, til the next morning. Oh yes the girls had got their dick back and they screamed as he shot their pussy's full. The girls were happy and kept the place clean and cooked meals for Ken, they loved to cook for Ken wearing only an apron, they showed their lovely titties. Ken screwed the girls at least twice each night through the week and more on weekends. After sometime passed Ken began to see a change in the girls and in the place. Ken watched as the place began to look and smell as it had before with the girls. They came home one evening and Ken met them at the door with an overnight bag. You going somewhere Ken Renae asked? Ken said girls I told you what I would do when you made a mess here again, yes I'm gone. Zenae said what about your clothes in our closet, when will you be back to get all you have here? Ken said you girls should call your Mom, you don't know how much she needs you now. Renae said it's like this, you and Mom can go for a long walk off of a short pier. He said girls I've met some people that were uncaring but they had no hope to be better. You two I don't believe have any care except what you want, now bye girls. The door closed as he left. Zenae said we got him Sis, yea. Ken went to his other place and went inside and sat his bag down. A light was on in the bathroom, the maid must have left it on he thought. Ken went to the bathroom and took a shower and got in bed but there was something wrong. First a loud scream then a woman began to cry. Please don't rape me I beg of you, I'm not a bad girl, oh please I beg you, don't hurt me. Ken got out of bed and turned the light on. Ken said Jasmine you were to be gone by now, what happened? Oh Ken I messed up, well sort of. Ken said here stop shaking it's all right, I won't hurt you. Oh Ken I'm a little scared but more excited. Ken I want to ask you and I don't know, do you have a large dick? Ken said a dick wasn't what we were talking about. Ken you are my only true friend that I have and you have helped me so much, Ken do friends screw? Ken said yes I guess that friends screw, now why are you still here? Ken my legs are shaking and I need to lay down. Go ahead honey and lay down, then tell me why you are still here. She lay down on the bed and my she was a lovely woman and he began to just stare at the beauty that was spread before him. Ken will you lay back down beside me? He said it might be the best if I stood here to talk. Ken do men and women talk naked as you are doing. Not all the time they don't he said. Well please lay down beside me. Jasmine had a near perfect body as any woman he had seen. Ken layed down beside of her and he could feel the heat from her lovely body. Ken I'm a little scared, will you hold me please. Ken put his arms around her and held her and she lay in his arms. Ken I've never had anything such as this before and I already love it. Ken said are you ready to tell me why you are still here in my place? Jasmine said Ken after I moved my clothes in here and started my job, I did as you said to do. I went to the shelter and met a nice lady that needed help as I had. She had a job but no clothes nor a place to live. So I kept enough of the money you gave me for my groceries and gave her the remainder for her clothes and rent. I was going to stay here til you came back or til I got payed. I got paid and went to pay my rent on my new place. The place had already been rented so I tried to find another place I could afford. Guess what I last saw you at your restaurant so I went back there to try to find you. Well I didn't and none of the workers had seen you since I had. Ken now I thought you may have took a long vacation or be away on a business trip, then I was informed in a polite way that my rent here was due,either pay or move on. Ken you have a nice place here but I believe you are being ripped off by the landlord. I had to count pennies to pay the rent. Ken said now I told you to call me if you ever needed me. Yes that's another thing, I lost your phone number then I lost my phone or someone stole it, Ken I'm so glad you came back. Now Ken tell me, do friends screw, well if they do I'm ready, even if they don't. Ken said Jasmine how much of this have you done before? You mean screwing or laying in a bed holding a dick? Either one he said. She said I told you about my two week deal I was screwed twice and he ran out on me and left me with nothing but a want to be screwed. Ken I told you before that I hadn't had but one dick twice and that's it. She said I have had only one dick and my pussy got hot and it never had before, so now can we screw Ken? Ken said Jasmine there's more to it than screwing. Yes I guess there must be so tell me all I need to know then screw my pussy. He said are you on birth control? Oh yes she said so what's next? He said if you are sure we will begin and I make love and then we screw. She said I better go wash my pussy it's wet. He said may I wash it for you? She said oh my Ken will you please, may I wash your dick for you? My dick's not wet he said. She said let's go and I get to wash your dick. She got to wash the first dick she had ever seen and she was ready to screw she said. Jasmine was a wild one in bed as Ken gave her what she was wanting and she gave a loud scream as she held her legs up as he shot her pussy full. Ken can a man do it more than one time in a week? Yes if a woman wants to screw she can.

Get your dick in my pussy when you can she said. Jasmine learned that she loved to screw but she loved to just lay in Ken's arms and run her hands all over his body. She loved the way Ken played with her body to build her up to a point that she had never thought she would be. When she got to that point to her it seemed that she was in a world of such pleasure that all else didn't matter. She loved all the pleasure she received but she loved it more when Ken got his pleasure. She hadn't seen but the one dick, Ken's and he filled her pussy with his dick and all else to her wasn't in her world. Ken still made his regular calls to Lenae and she said Ken those two girls are up to something so watch out. He said oh they will be wanting me to bring my dick back to them soon. She said now Jasmine can take care of your dick for me and don't worry about those two girls and their pussy's. Ken said I miss you and yes she said I miss you too. Time passed and

Jasmine was now using her pussy on Ken's dick the way she had dreamed of using her pussy. She was a wild woman in bed to be so quiet, but not in bed. Ken started in his office one morning and his receptionist said Mr. Brewster is in your office, he just got here. Ken went in and Dan Brewster was standing looking over some papers. Ken said Dan what brings you here so early? He said Ken there's several reasons why I'm here but first I have a DVD to show you so take a seat and no comments til it plays through. The DVD played and at first Ken didn't know what the DVD was about. He wondered how what the DVD showed that concerned him. Dan said you saw all of what was going on at your place with those two girls. Ken said but you never saw me in the DVD even with one girl, so what's the deal? Dan said first the deal is that as one of her lovers is in bed screwing one of the girls it seems and the other man comes in the door her lover has left unlocked. Ken we didn't know about this, or the company didn't until the hotel alerted us. Our detective looked over the hotel tapes and went to each one of these girl's departments and they saw and identified the girl's lovers. The girls took their lovers from their own workplace to their place on different days. Ken as you can see one man is going through your papers you were taking home. Ken we have lost out to our rivals because of this. The girls departments were never up to our standards and I hoped you would catch it. Now I don't care about how much you screw but not with our own employees. You know you can't, that's never been tolerated. Dan said Ken this is a case of corporate espionage and my attorney's are on top of all of this. Dan said as of now there are the two white men and two blacks from our company being arrested and charged with corporate espionage. The ones that actually took our company records from your place have already been arrested and charged as the other four men. Dan said the worst part, the Peters girl's have you accused of sexual harassment on and off the job. He said the girls say you forced them to have sex with you or they would lose their jobs. Our attorney's asked for dates and places of all this occurred, yes right in your bed they said. The girls are real smart Ken. They produced one of the sheets from your bed for a DNA test. Yes the sheet was nasty and had plenty of the girls DNA. Yes also all four of the other four men that were in bed with the girls. You had a break from screwing the girls, no DNA belonged to you. We doubled all the DNA tests. Ken the girls nor their attorney Miss Ellen Mantridge doesn't know about the DNA test that I had tested. Now Ken this is a mess that you have let get to this point. Yes I know how you go overboard to help all of the people that you can but this is business. Ken those two girls have been, along with their lovers selling company plans right out of their departments. Ken their attorney says she will win in court but I don't want this to get in court. The board of directors have met and all have decided that you have to go. I relieve you now of any and all ties with this company. He said Ken this isn't these two girls first rodeo that I supposedly learned, but their attorney doesn't know this or doesn't care. Ken those girls caused a good professor in college to lose his position because those two filed sexual harassment charges on the man. The school payed out a large sum of money to keep them two quiet. The Professor lost his position at the college and also lost his wife and children. Ken I don't care now how this goes but I will let you put it on the line to those girls. They can go on with this sexual harassment case and I'll have them both arrested and charged as it is with their lovers and the others involved. Ken all are looking at a ten or twenty year sentence plus damages paid to my company. I will have the girls and their attorney brought in and they can listen to themselves scream as we are being robbed of our plans. Dan said it's up to you as what you do but I can't see much of a future for those girls, they will never work east of the Mississippi for sure. Ken said do you mean to show the DVD to the girls? Yes and we had a court orders for all of your place to be filmed and set up recording equipment that their attorney doesn't know about and I'll inform her of such. Dan pressed the intercom and said please send in Miss Mantridge and her clients. Soon the girls and their attorney were in the office. Dan said Miss Mantridge to begin I don't know how much background work you did on your clients but this is part of their record, look it over, I have a DVD for you three to watch and yes my attorney's had court orders to film and record all of this. Now here we go and listen ladies to the sound as it fits in to what you were doing at the time, let's begin. The girls watched as they led their lovers into their place as the other man went over Ken's papers as the girls screwed or so it sounded by them. Dan said ladies that's it. Miss Mantridge said so the girls were in bed, maybe with a good lover. Dan said Miss those lovers as you say are the girls department workers. Ma'am those men along with your clients have been stealing company secrets, you say from their place to their workplace. They went to far in this when they yelled sexual harassment as they have. Ma'am to make it plain I have attorney's waiting for my call to attain warrants for your clients arrest to be so charged with corporate espionage. Now I know you as a woman's right advocate but this case isn't as such. Miss your sexual harassment case won't hold up. The DNA on the sheets proved the girls were screwing four of the lovers but

not Ken as they accused. No
Mr. Brewster you are right, girls I have
no more to do with you in your case,
I've quit, oh yes girls cut a deal if you
can with Mr. Brewster. She got up and
left the office, Ken said ladies do you
have another attorney on your case?
No Renae said but what about our
DNA test on your sheet Ken?
Ken said you girls got messed up on
that because I had left when you took
all of your lovers to bed, all of you and
your lovers DNA was on the sheet not
mine. Renae said I was sure we got our
time right for Ken's DNA to be on the
sheet. Zenae said I guess you messed
up, no you did, no you did, no you did.
Mr. Brewster said Ken I've got some
business in private with you but I'll talk
about it in another office. Well girls I
hope you are happy with your plans.
Now I'm going out for a minute while you
two can plot some more in private. Ken
went to another office and he couldn't
believe the girls were so cool in all of

this. After some time he went back to where the girls sat with smug looks on their faces. Well Ken are you ready to settle with me and Sis out of court, we may let you get some of our pussy too. Ken said girls I have no power to what the company will do but I know if you go to court on any of these cases you will lose. If you do choose to take your case on you will probably get a ten to twenty year sentence for corporate espionage and all others the company attorney's can come up with. Zenae said but Ken you can stop them you are the CEO. Ken said I was the CEO, now thanks to you girls I'll never work for any company again when it's found out I let two smart ass girls try to extort my company. Yes girls I hope you have saved money while I paid all the bills. Renae said we paid for some of them. Ken said girls I see no future for you two anywhere, surely not back east. Now I made some calls to my friends and I got you both set up for a job interviews and here's the phone numbers and the address of each company. Renae said why do we both need the same address and phone number? Ken said look at the papers and you will see they aren't the same. Now if you can read you will see it's not the same company nor the same state. Yes you will be about three states apart if you do choose to go. Renae said we don't have the funds to get set up in another job in another state. Ken said girls that's your problem but what have you done with all of your money from the sale of Bob's place and your earnings here? Zenae said we did have a heart and Deone's little girl needed medical care and we paid it for him. Yes Renae said Devone's Mother she was dying of cancer and after her treatments Devone had ran out of funds. Well he had to put her in a nursing home that I payed for. Ken said you two are the smartest dumb assed girls I've ever met, or I hope to ever meet. Ken said you girls must not have ever looked at a company employee record. This Devone, his birth Mother died in child birth and he was adopted. His adopted Mother was killed by a stray bullet in a bar shoot out when he was in high school. Deone has no children nor any dependents at all on his record here. Now Deone's Mother has been dead for several years so they neither had a living Mother. Ken said I guess that's why they can afford to drive a Lamborghini to work and you girls ride a taxi as I did. Ken said girls I'm through here with you two as I have never had any say with you girls. Mr. Brewster will take your answer of whether you go to work here or in a prison laundry or kitchen. Ken had been getting all he had at the office in a box. Girls as of now I don't care but some day you should call your Mom. I know you haven't talked to her since I took you to see her and she's your Mother and she misses you, now bye, you big asses, or little. Zenae said hold it Ken we're not through with you. Renae said Ken how do you feel knowing you ate our pussy's just after Devone and Deone's big dick had just came out of our pussy's? Ken said I don't guess you two ever washed your pussy's did you? Now girls you are doing as you know to do. You try to justify your actions by a reaction like when I gave the lady at the shelter money for clothes and a room where she would feel good and look good for her job interview which she got the job. Yes and like when you accused me of eating Dawn's pussy also like when you accused me of raping your Mother. You girls try to justify your actions by a reaction. All I ever did for you I did because I love you two, not because you have had a good pussy and I said had, now it's rotten I guess. The worst you girls have done was to accuse a college professor of rape. The man lost his whole family and killed himself. He left a note that read the Peters girls lied, both girls yelled we didn't do that. Now girls how did my dick taste when you both sucked me off after I had just pulled my dick out of a street woman's pussy and her ass too, I never washed it either. Ken went home and took a long shower and lay down in the bed to think of what he would do next. Jasmine had found a place with his help that she could afford. Jasmine had learned how to make love and she had went wild for his dick. She told Ken that when his dick went up in her pussy that it pushed aside the past deal that she had got from her two screwings and made her want more of his dick. Ken lay and made his plans for what he had to do. He got up and cooked their meal for the evening. He heard Jasmine enter the place and yelled out, honey I'm home or we are. Ken looked and there stood Jasmine and another woman. She said Ken meet Shannon, I found her on the street with no place to go, well she was going to the homeless shelter but, well here we are, I hope you aren't mad at me. Ken she hasn't had a shower since she was kicked out of her place three days ago, but she doesn't stink, well not yet. Oh yes someone stole her luggage as she dozed off asleep. Guess what Ken they got her ID's and what little money she had. Ken she needs a shower and we are the same size so she wears my clothes for now. She said come on Shannon I'll show you around the place, oh I have to pee, you talk to Ken while I go pee. Ken said Miss where are you from if you care to say. Shannon said I don't care to say, I'm from a Midwest state if it matters. Ken said yes it does matter if we are to get your ID's back. Shannon said oh I thought you had other reasons to want to know about me. Ken said no as long as you aren't a murderer on the run. Oh no I've never hurt anyone or anything in my life. Jasmine yelled Shannon go wash off or shower. She said I put you a gown and panty's in the bathroom, now we sleep naked, don't we Ken. Yes he said we do. While Shannon took a long shower Jasmine said Ken I had to help her but there's something else wrong so tell me. Ken told her all he could of what all went wrong for him that day. She said and those girls did you like that after all you have done to help them, now I have to help Shannon get up on her feet if you don't throw both of us out first. Ken all I know about her is that she has screwed some before she came to this city, but like me she never got her pussy hurt with a dick. Yes she's on birth control, now isn't that real nice for you Ken? Oh heck Ken I blabbed about what a lover your are and she was ready to screw you before we got here. Ken if you will, please make her feel good about herself and make her pussy feel good, like tonight maybe. Ken you know the deal about my new place and I can't move until this weekend. Shannon's to go to work tomorrow at her new job and I hope you will let her stay with us til I move out, then she stays with me til she gets her own place. Ken what she needs the most is your love and your large dick. Ken I will never forget what you and your love and large dick has done for me and my pussy. Ken please show her some love and give her the one screwing she will never forget. Ken she says that after some bad deals she hasn't been screwed in over four years and I believe her, oh here she comes. Ken isn't she a lovely angel and she looks better now that she has took a shower, my Shannon you sure do look nice doesn't she Ken? Yes Ken said she's a very lovely lady, now let's eat. After they ate their meal and cleaned up the kitchen Jasmine said I'm going to take my shower. She said Shannon I'll let you and Ken get to know each other and I'll meet both of you in bed, naked. After Jasmine went to take her shower

Shannon said Mr. Marshall none of this was my idea. Now Jasmine and I just met today and I may have led her to think I had a hot pussy and was ready for a dick. I've been screwed twice by different dicks. The first one got my virginity when I was twelve years old and it hurt and scared my ass off. I would never have another dick in my pussy. That worked out real well til I went through all my schooling and got my degrees that I wanted and a job. My Mother died during this time. I met a young man through a fellow at work and we hit it off and yes we screwed once and it hurt my pussy bad. He said he would be gone on a business trip for a week. The business trip was a big drug deal up north that went bad and he was killed. Somehow word got back to Dad that I was screwing the fellow. Dad kicked me out of our house and he let my boss know that I was involved with a drug dealer and that I was on drugs. I lost all I had and my job and

I had to leave home with nothing nearly. I've never done drugs, nor alcohol, no sex. Now I may have led Jasmine to believe that I'm hot for a dick, I'm not. If it comes to it and you screw my pussy please don't hurt me. Yes she asked if I had ever done a threesome and I said why sure haven't you, at the time I didn't think I would be standing with you or any man talking about it. Jasmine yelled I'm in the bed ready for you two so let's move it now. Ken said I have to take a pee and wash my dick. Yes Shannon said me too, well not my dick but my pussy, come on Mr. Marshall let's go take our pee and I'll let you wash my pussy and I'll wash your dick. Shannon said close the bathroom door and let me see your dick before you wash my pussy. Oh my Ken I've never believed a dick would be so large, will he hurt my pussy when he goes in? He said we haven't got to that part yet. No she said but I know that I want your dick in my pussy and I'll help all I know how.

Now Ken was in bed with two lovely women that wanted to screw. Jasmine said Ken screw her pussy first and give her a hard one. Ken had Shannon's pussy hot and ready when he eased his large dick in her pussy as she gave out a gasp. She soon had it all up in her pussy and he gave her one that she would never forget. He made it last for near a half an hour before he shot her pussy full and she gave out a loud squeal. Oh my what you made me and my pussy feel, oh I have to kiss you, can we do it some more after Jasmine gets hers? Ken said if you want we may can do it some more tonight. Jasmine got her screwing and Shannon watched and seemed to like to watch Jasmine shake her ass and work her pussy to help Ken til she let out a loud scream. Shannon said I'm ready to screw when you can Ken and I'll shake my ass for you this time. She more than shook her ass, she rolled her pussy up and down his dick til she milked him dry. Jasmine said we better go wash our pussy's before we mess up the bed. Ken said you want me to wash your pussy's? Shannon said yes as Jasmine said no we will wash them. Jasmine came back to bed alone and said Ken there's something I must tell you now. Ken when I saw Shannon's pussy as you ate it I got excited and my pussy got hot. Now I don't know about this and I've never been like this before. Ken I got jealous of you and Shannon. Ken I wanted to eat her pussy and still do, Ken I don't know why but I love her and I need to eat her pussy and love her. Ken leave her alone she's all mine, pussy wise. Now Ken what do you think of this? Ken said it's not what I may think but what will Shannon think of this. Oh Ken I don't want to make her mad, heck I love her and I have never felt like this for a woman, now do you think it would be right for me to eat her pussy? Ken said I don't think it would be right for you to eat any woman's pussy. Ken she said I don't want you to screw her any more, please. Ken said you are the one that asked me to screw her. Yes that was before I saw her pussy and watched you eat her pussy. Ken said I will let you and Shannon work this matter out and I'll be moving up state after I help get Shannon's ID's process started. Shannon came back to bed and said I'm ready now, I've got a clean pussy for you Ken and I want your large dick in it now. Jasmine said Shannon we've worked Ken's dick to hard on our first screw so we have to let his dick rest. Yes I went wild I guess Shannon said, it had been a long time ago for me to screw. The next morning Ken told the girls bye. Shannon said we will see you   after work today? No Ken said after I get your ID process started I'll be moving on. You check with Jasmine about your ID's, I gave her address to where your new ID's will be mailed to. Shannon said Ken I loved your dick and the way it made me and my pussy feel. Jasmine said Shannon Ken has a lot to do and a long drive today so bye Ken. Shannon said bye Ken and I love you. Ken took care of all he needed to do and he left New York City behind him. Ken wondered about Renae and Zenae if they had made up their mind to leave the city also. He knew they hadn't talked to their Mom since he took the road trip with them. The only thing he was leaving behind was Uncle Bob's old place and a lot of good and bad memories. Ken went up the walkway and rang the doorbell. After a few minutes the door opened, she stood for a moment. She said oh my love and was upon his waist going wild kissing him. She said it's been so long but it's worth the wait. She said come on I've got your room ready and I said your room. He said Lenae have the girls called you? She said Ken let's not worry about our girls, as if it would matter. Ken I've got a hot pussy for you as I had the first time we met. Now I won't pressure you but you know the plan so no pussy from me til it's right. Ken said I've got me a good honest woman that I love. She said Ken you know all we did the first time, well my pussy is wet but I'll go wash it as you wash your dick, then let's cheat a little or a lot. Soon Ken was washing her hot pussy. She said Ken I believe your dick has got a lot bigger since our first time. He said I guess your brats screwing me helped it to grow. Let's go she said and Ken and Lenae were wed the next week and took a short honeymoon. Lenae had disposed of all she owned some time back and she moved into the mansion. With help the mansion was made to be a bed and breakfast, with mostly help from the homeless shelter. She had a good business going. Ken stayed busy helping as he could at the mansion. He hoped that the little assed girls would call some day. He thought about all the help he gave them as they were plotting and planning. Lenae had said they were connivers and now he believed her. Jasmine and Shannon were all one in all they do, they lived as one also. Hey Ken I've got it ready for you so come on and get all you want. Ken would never get all he wanted from his lovely woman and it got better each time. The saying as he thought like Daughter's like Mother, no the Mother was the best for now. Years passed and Lenae sat in her office and had checked her registration book for the bed and breakfast that she was operating. She was so happy that Ken had trusted in her to give her complete control of the business. He said it gave him more time to do what he loves to do as he was doing today and that was to visit and work at the homeless shelters. Ken loved to meet and help those that wanted his help. He knew that there were many that only wanted a place to stay and a free meal for a while and then they would move on. He knew some that wanted a change in their life and would work if they could only get a break. Ken could help them get a big break they would need to start a new life for themselves. Lenae's phone rang and she answered and said yes I have them booked but they are early, thanks Carla and I will go greet them as I do with all of our guests. She went to the front entrance of the mansion and Carla was still with the early guests. She said Carla you may go about your regular duties I will take care of these two. She said now why are you two here after all this time? Zenae said Mom we are here for more than one reason. One we have our room reserved for each one of us for seven days and nights. No Lenae said I don't have you on my register so you may forget about a room here at all. Zenae said Mom I am registered under the name of Margie Pickett and my Sister's name is Sophie Foster or that's the name we gave you when we made our reservation. Zenae said Mom that's one reason why we are here at your home. Mom I'm here to say I'm sorry for all we have done to hurt you since you began calling me a brat. Mom I'm here to try to tell Ken, the only man I have ever loved that I'm sorry for all I have ever done to hurt him, Mom he deserved better and he's got you, and that covers most of why we are here. Lenae said Renae what's wrong with you that you're not running your bratty ass mouth as usual as your Sister Zenae has been doing? Zenae said Mom please don't call us brats, yes we have been bitches to you and Ken and others. Mom Renae has a problem that she doesn't wish to speak to you about at this time, it's sort of like something that happened to us or mostly Renae when we were your young brats. Zenae said Mom I'm sorry about arriving here early and we will try to get a taxi to pick us up and take us back to town and come back at a suitable time for you, if there may be one. No Lenae said I'll find a place for you somewhere here in the mansion. Zenae said yes just like old times at home when you wanted to do the things you liked to do. Yes we were just put out of your way in our room. Mom I guess that's when and how Renae and I began to plot and plan and became your bratty ass girls as you called us. Mom it took years before we figured out what you were doing in your room with the delivery man that stopped at our house at least three times each week and he never brought one package in the house with him. Zenae said Sis I see the taxi I called for us is here so let's ride back to town. Lenae said you don't have to leave, and what do you know about this delivery man? Zenae said Mom we may have been brats but we weren't dumb. Oh yes one more reason I'm here is I'm going to screw Ken again if he will screw me, now go tidy up my room and Renae's that we have paid for in advance, and as your ad says no refunds except in emergency's, let's go Sis and do something worth while with our time and again Mom I'm sorry for all I have done to hurt you. Yes now I know why you had a bad need as you did as we were your little ass brats. Yes Mom you weren't getting screwed by Dad because he was busy at work, just slowly working himself to death, let's go Sis. Later that evening the girls were in their separate rooms at the mansion when a knock came at Zenae's door. Ken come on in and please sit down, now I've told you many times that I'm sorry of the way I treated you and I'll let my Sis apologize herself and I'm sure she will. Ken thanks for all you have done for me and my Sis and you know there's something else I want you to do that we have talked about on the phone. Ken said yes and you are asking a lot from me and your Mom. Oh Ken I'm sure you will do it for us and it all will be as good as ever. Ken you do know that me and Sis were being drugged when you thought we were in on the stealing company secrets. Ken we weren't even screwing anyone but you, but it looked like we were. Ken Sis and I were brats but our pussy's were all yours, I swear. Ken, Mom loves you and I do also but I love you for being the first man to ever show me any love. Ken the first time you made love with me and later screwed my Sis, I got jealous because you screwed her and I was never like that before, I mean jealous of her for anything. Ken I just wanted you all for myself and I find it hard now to even think of you and Mom screwing. Ken we have discussed this over the phone and yes I do get hot even thinking about it. Now you have helped Sis and I get positions at the homeless shelters in two different towns as administrators, but you know what else we want and need. Ken Renae has a real serious problem that I want you to see if she will talk to you about. She has to have help or I think she will just go away and not come back, please help her. Ken you can tell Mom what I want or not because I want to do this for myself and Mom if she wants to. Ken I'm ready to start on our plan when you want me, like right now, here I am it's only been for you my love. My Zenae you are as lovely as I remember, not one flaw on your lovely body. Oh my Ken let's do it now for all you want. Oh yes Ken how I've cried and longed for you and your love. Oh Zenae you are as you were the first time we made love. Ken if I hadn't been on birth control before when we did it I know you would have got me pregnant. Ken you are still filling it up with your juices and you make it feel so good when it fills up and runs back out all around it and my butt, Ken I love you so much. Ken I'm not sure Renae will want you to screw her because she's had some real bad problems that I can't tell you about but I'm hoping she will talk to you. Ken if she doesn't talk to you I'm afraid she will go away in her mind and never come back. Ken I believe she wants to screw you but in her mind she's afraid to do it over something that has happened to her. Ken she loves you I know because she, like me have only had one lover and that was you. Ken it all felt good before and now what you gave me was the best any woman will have inside of her. Ken do it once more before you go and I'll be ready for you anytime you want to do it, yes please try Renae's tomorrow night if you will, now give me all you have got. The next night Renae opened her door and said please come in and sit down. First Ken I want to tell you I'm sorry for all the trouble I've caused you. Ken I love you for one, you were my first love and you have been my last true love. Ken I have a bad problem that I feel like you are the only person that can help me with, I'll try to tell you this. Now as of now there's only three people that know of this. You know you sent Zenae and me to different cities in different started work. After some time Sis and I found each other by social media, it's called. I had got myself up to where I could date a fellow and I did. He was a nice fellow and so easy going, a well built hunky type man. We dated for a few months and I had said no sex to him. He asked me over to his place to watch a football game that was on TV. It was soon an all out fight with him to keep my pants and panty's on. I told him I was going home which wasn't far, I had walked to his place. He went into a wild rage like I had never seen in anyone before. He was trying to rape me and I put up a fight. Ken he beat me nearly to death and then he pulled me up off the floor by my hair and dragged me by my hair to the door and shoved me out on the walk and left me there. I somehow got myself home and got my torn blood soaked clothes off and done the only thing I knew to do. I did as I had done with Zenae when we were little girls back in our neighborhood as we were out playing with our friends. Ken this boy asked me and Sis if we wanted to see some baby rabbits. Sure we wanted to look at the baby rabbits. He said they were in a rabbit nest back in the woods and all that wanted to pet a baby rabbit to follow him. Sis and I were the only ones to follow him into the woods away from all the houses. He stopped and then he had Zenae down on the grass and pulled her dress up and he was trying to pull her panty's down. I did all I knew to do at the time, and I jumped on his back and hit at his face. He was a big boy and he soon had me down on the ground. I had never seen what a boy had down there and I had seen what Sis and I had. He tried again to put what he had in Sis as she cried. Now I guess he must have had a big one, or it was to me, it looked big. As he was trying to hurt Sis I kicked him in a place where it must have hurt him. He came after me and then threw me on the ground and pulled my pants and panty's down and I kicked and screamed as he did something down there and it hurt. He hadn't done as he tried to do but he pushed his long finger up in my little girl place as I screamed. It was then that Zenae gave him a hard kick between his legs as he yelled. He said some words that we hadn't ever heard before and left us on our asses. He had whipped our little asses as he called us and left us bleeding. We sneaked in our house not knowing what to tell Mom. There was a delivery truck in front of our house as had been for several different times before even when we got no packages. We started to our room when we heard Mom yell out I want it all now. Sis and I were dumb so we got some clothes and went to take a long bath. Yes I guess the boy hurt me bad down there but I would never know because I was just Mom's brat. When I got beat by my so called friend out west I couldn't tell anyone but Sis and she took off from her work and came and helped me get over the beating he gave me. Ken I can't blame Mom for what has happened to me but I've never felt like I was wanted by anyone except you. Dad was always busy at work or at home. Ken I want to give myself to you as I did the first time in the big city, oh yes you know what else I want you to do for me. Ken said are you sure you want to do this? Renae said Ken you see all I have to offer you and you didn't wear it out before and it's still as you left it my love. Oh my Ken you are still the best looking man I know. Now give me all you have my love and I'll be all I can for you. Oh my Ken that feels so good up in me, now my one and only lover I will give all of myself to you. Oh Ken that feels so good up in me so deep just like it always felt.

Oh my love you have been my only one love and most likely will still always be my only love. Yes I love it when you rub my back and butt the way you always did. Ken you still are shooting out the biggest load of juice ever and I hope all of our plans work out for all of us, Mom too. The girls got their wishes on their first visit to Lenae's bed and breakfast it seemed. They were happy to give Ken something he had never had before. Yes Zenae gave birth to her girl and a few days later Renae gave birth to her boy. Ken was as proud as he could be, Lenae said that both of the baby's looked like Ken and she was proud to be a Grandma. The girls understood now about the delivery man and why their Mom did a lot of screaming at the times she was in her bedroom with the delivery man. Did the girl's feel bad about screwing their Mom's husband? No not at all and they still get it when they can from the only lover they have ever known or most likely ever will know. Ken loves to make all three girls happy which he can and will continue doing.

The End of
Daughters like Mother